A KILLER ~~HUR~~ THE GUNSMITH!

He drew his gun and turned in one motion. The flash of the killer's gun had barely faded when Clint fired. The killer was turning back to Clint, but not nearly in time. Clint's bullet hit the man in the hip, turning him around completely. He staggered away a few feet, bent over, trying to stay on his feet. . . .

He might have been able to slip away to try and evade capture, but instead of trying he forced himself to turn and face Clint. He brought his gun up, and Clint fired again. . . .

*   *   *

SPECIAL PREVIEW!

Turn to the back of this book for an exciting excerpt from the blazing new series . . .

Desperado

THE GUNSMITH

136

VALLEY MASSACRE

J. R. ROBERTS

JOVE BOOKS, NEW YORK

VALLEY MASSACRE

A Jove Book / published by arrangement with
the author

PRINTING HISTORY
Jove edition / April 1993

ISBN: 0-515-11084-1

Jove Books are published by The Berkley Publishing Group,
200 Madison Avenue, New York, New York 10016.
The name "JOVE" and the "J" logo
are trademarks belonging to Jove Publications, Inc.

PRINTED IN THE UNITED STATES OF AMERICA

10 9 8 7 6 5 4 3 2 1

THE GUNSMITH

136

VALLEY MASSACRE

ONE

When Clint stepped off the train at Philadelphia's 36th Street Station he was still shaking his head. Once again he was being called on to perform a service for the United States Secret Service, and once again he had agreed to do so. Sometimes he was just so patriotic that he scared himself.

Actually, patriotism was just one part of it. If each and every one of these requests had not come directly from his friend Jim West, he probably could have turned them down—some of them, at least.

For West's part, some people might say that the man was taking advantage of his friendship with Clint Adams, but Clint himself didn't feel that way. He understood that West *was* acting purely from patriotism. Jim West felt it was his duty to do whatever he had to do for his country, and if that meant *maybe* taking advantage of his friendship with Clint Adams, then that's what the man would do.

Clint Adams had a history—a strong history—of dropping anything he was doing when a friend called on him for help. West, being one of his best friends, was especially deserving of whatever help Clint could give him.

Still, Clint couldn't help looking around him, wondering what the hell he was doing in Philadelphia. . . .

He had gone to Washington, D.C., first. As was usually the case, Jim West wasn't available to see him. Invariably, when West called on him for help it was because he himself had to be somewhere else. Consequently he was rarely around to explain the situation himself. The last time Clint had agreed to work for the Secret Service it had been West's partner, Russ Martin, who met with him. In this case Clint knew he was going to have to meet with the head of the Secret Service himself, William Masters Cartwright.

Cartwright and Clint disliked each other . . . intensely. Clint thought Cartwright was a useless politician, and Cartwright thought Clint was a disrespectful braggart. Both men were wrong, but neither would ever admit it.

Clint checked into his hotel, the D.C. House, and then went directly to Cartwright's office on K Street. Cartwright was waiting in his office, seated behind his big oak desk.

"Well, Adams," he said as Clint entered, "thanks for coming on such short notice."

Clint was in the act of sitting and stopped short, staring at Cartwright. Was it possible? Was the man being civil? Clint sat down, still eyeing Cartwright warily. The man must have something up his sleeve.

"I came as soon as I got Jim West's message," Clint said.

"Ah, yes, our Mr. West," Cartwright said, folding his hands on the top of his desk. "As usual, he's a busy man."

"If he wasn't," Clint said, "I wouldn't be here, would I?"

"No, no," Cartwright said, "of course not. I know that the only reason you're here is that Jim West asked you to come. I understand that."

"Good," Clint said. "So tell me what the problem is this time."

"The problem," Cartwright said, "is a grave threat to the President of the United States. . . ."

"I see."

"Maybe."

Clint frowned.

"What do you mean, maybe?"

"I mean," Cartwright said, "that we have *heard* that there might be some sort of . . . of a . . . a *plot* being hatched by . . . by *someone*—"

"It doesn't sound like you *know* a heck of a lot of anything, do you?" Clint asked.

"Well . . . not actually, no," Cartwright said. "We've heard some rumblings that there might possibly be something as heinous as an assassination being planned, but no, you're quite right. We're not sure."

"And I'm here to make sure?"

"Yes," Cartwright said. "We've received word from an informant that he will talk to a single agent, passing on what he knows, for a guarantee of no charges being filed against him, personally."

"All right," Clint said, "I'll talk to him. I don't

know why you couldn't have one of your other agents handle this, though. If it's just a matter of *talking*—"

"He asked for you."

Clint stopped short.

"What?"

"The man asked specifically for you."

"Does he know that I've done some work for you before?" Clint asked.

Cartwright spread his hands.

"We don't know," he said.

"Well, who is he?"

"We don't know that, either."

"And he asked for me?"

Cartwright nodded and said, "Specifically."

Clint rubbed his jaw and said, "I don't like the sound of that."

"Why not?"

"Well, it could be a setup."

"You mean someone wanted you so badly that they made up a story about an assassination attempt on the President of the United States?" Cartwright asked.

"Not when you put it that way," Clint said, "but I am a rather popular target, given my past . . . reputation." Clint hated using that word.

"Past reputation?" Cartwright repeated, and for a moment Clint thought that the old Cartwright was coming back. Actually, he would have welcomed the old Cartwright. He was very wary of this new, civil version.

"Yes," Clint said, "past reputation."

"Well," Cartwright said, "I can send someone with you, if you like—"

"No, that's all right," Clint said, holding up his hand. "That is, unless you're offering me West or Russ Martin?"

"I'm afraid both of those gentlemen are on assignments at the present time."

"Then I'll go it alone, thanks," Clint said. "Tell me, where do I meet this informant, and how will I know him?"

"He'll know you," Cartwright said, looking at the ceiling, "and you're to meet him in . . . Philadelphia."

"Philadelphia?"

TWO

Clint had never been to Philadelphia before. Outside the station he approached a horse-drawn cab and caught the dozing driver's attention. The man almost fell from his perch, then dropped down to accept Clint's carpetbag. He was in his early twenties and had a quick and infectious grin.

"Where can I take you, sir?" he asked.

"I need a hotel," Clint said.

"What hotel, sir?"

"I don't know," Clint said. "Something reasonable, but not *too* cheap, and with good food."

The man's grin widened and he said, "I know just the place."

"One that doesn't give you a dollar a head for guests you steer their way?" Clint asked.

"Sir," the man said, "you wound me. I only do that for *two* dollars a head."

"Oh, I see."

"But I wouldn't take you there if it wasn't a good hotel," the man swore.

"I'm sure."

"And it does have good food."

"All right."

"And a pretty waitress or two."

"Now you've talked me into it," Clint said. "Let's go."

On the way he found out that the young man's name was Bob Lester.

"You can call me Les," he said. "Most people do."

"Why not Bob?"

The man made a face and said, "There are lots of Bobs, aren't there?"

"You have a point."

"What's your name?"

"Clint."

The man thought a moment and then said, "Not too many Clints, I don't think—not in the East, anyway."

On the way to the hotel the man pointed out the sights, including the Liberty Bell, which was only a couple of blocks from the hotel, which was on Arch Street.

"Maybe I'll walk over and have a look at it later," Clint said.

"Ever been to Philly before? Philly, that's what I call it."

"Sounds catchy," Clint said. "No, I've never been here before."

"Been to other cities?"

"Oh, sure. New York, San Francisco, New Orleans, Washington, Denver—"

"You get around."

"I travel some, yeah."

"Well, this is just like any other big city," Les said. "I mean, it's my home, but there's really nothing here you can't get in any of those places."

"Except the Liberty Bell."

"Well . . . you know what I mean," Les said.

"Sure," Clint said, and he did. Les was telling him—in his own way—that if he wanted to gamble, or if he wanted a girl, Les could help him with it. "I know exactly what you mean."

"I knew you would."

Les dropped Clint at the Holiday Hotel. It was a moderate structure, but it was clean and in a good neighborhood. Les assured Clint that it wasn't too expensive.

"If you've got expensive tastes for *anything*," the young man added, "just let me know."

"And how will I find you?"

Les grinned and said, "Oh, that's easy. Just tell the desk clerk. He's my cousin."

Clint watched Les climb aboard his cab and drive away, then turned and went into the hotel. He was *real* glad that Les had been so emotionally uninvolved in choosing a hotel.

He went up to the front desk and put his bag down on the floor. The desk clerk turned, gave him an infectious grin, and said, "Can I help you?"

"Uh, yeah, I need a room."

"Yes, sir," the man said, reversing the register. "Just sign in there, and I'll be happy to take care of you. How did you hear about our establishment?"

"Your cousin, Bob Lester—" was as far as Clint got.

"That thief?" the man said. "If he thinks I'm paying him anything, he's got another thought coming, I tell you that."

"But he said—"

"Never mind what he said," the clerk told Clint. "I'm sorry, sir, it's just that Les is sort of the black sheep of our family. I'm sorry if he made promises—"

"He said it was a nice hotel with good food," Clint said.

The man looked shocked.

"Is that what he said?" he asked. "Is that all he said?"

"Well . . . he did say that you might have a pretty waitress or two."

The man looked aggrieved.

"Jesus, he didn't offer any of them to you, did he?" he asked.

"No, of course not," Clint said.

"Well, that's a relief," the man said. He turned the register back around and read, "Mr. Adams, from Washington. I'm sorry, Mr. Adams. I'm going to give you one of our very best rooms for the inconvenience."

"There was no inconvenience—"

"And I'm sorry you had to meet Les," he said. "My name is Harold. I have the unfortunate distinction of sharing my last name with that . . . that rogue!"

"Can I get someone to take my bag up to my room?" Clint asked.

"Of course, sir," Harold said. "Is there anything else I can do for you?"

"Just have my bag brought up to my room, tell me what room it is, give me my key, and point to the dining room."

The tone of Clint's voice must have given away the fact that he didn't care for Harold Lester.

"Very well, sir," Harold said. "Front!"

An older gentleman in a bellhop's uniform came over.

"Take Mr. Adams's bag up to room 207," Harold said. He handed Clint the key. "The dining room is right over there, sir," Harold told him, pointing to the right.

"Thanks."

"Sir?"

Clint turned.

"Yes?"

"Have I offended you in some way?"

"Harold," Clint said, "it just seems to me that you could take some lessons from that 'rogue' cousin of yours."

"Sir?"

"Never mind."

Clint walked away from the front desk. He just knew that he could meet every other member of Les's family, and he'd still rather spend time with the "black sheep" than all of the others put together—if the others were anything like Harold.

THREE

As it turned out, Les had been telling the truth. The food in the dining room was fine, and the waitress who served it was young and pretty. No beauty, but pretty, and as an added bonus, the coffee was good. Strong and black, just the way he liked it.

"Anything else, sir?" she asked after he had finished his second pot of coffee.

"No," he said, "the meal was fine, just fine."

"Thank you, sir."

"I'm in room 207," he said, standing up. "Would you see that the meal goes on my bill?"

"Of course, sir."

"Here," he said, handing her a dollar, "this is for you."

"Thank you, sir," she said. "I hope you enjoy your stay here."

"I hope so, too," he said.

It wasn't late, but he didn't feel much like leaving the hotel. He decided to go up to his room and turn in early.

"My name's Alison," the waitress said as he started walking toward the lobby.

He turned and looked at her. She wasn't very big, about five one or two, and she was slender—skinny, even. Her hair was brown and long, although it was tied back so it wouldn't get in her way while she worked. She had straight eyebrows, an equally straight nose, and thin lips. She was quite young, probably twenty-two or -three.

"You're very pretty, Alison," he said to her, and then turned and left.

His room was on the second floor of the three-story building. It was fairly large, larger than most rooms he'd stayed in, not as large as some others he'd seen in New York and Denver. He walked to the window and saw that it overlooked the front of the hotel, on Arch Street.

His carpetbag was on the bed. He removed it, dropped it to the floor, and sat on the bed to take off his boots. That done, he stood and removed his gun belt, hanging it on the bedpost. He slipped off his shirt, then his pants, and finally laid down on the bed.

Tomorrow there would be time enough to go out and take a look at Philadelphia, maybe sightsee a bit, even see the Liberty Bell. His instructions were to walk around, anyway, and wait to be contacted. He could do whatever he wanted to do, eat, drink, gamble, frequent any kind of establishment he wanted to. . . .

"Just don't hole up in the hotel, Adams," Cartwright had said. "Be out where he can see you. When he's satisfied that you're alone, and it's safe to approach you, he'll make contact."

"And just how long am I supposed to wait?" Clint had asked.

"As long as it takes, Mr. Adams," Cartwright said. "You can't rush this sort of thing. We don't want our man to spook and run. If he does, we may never know what's being planned until after it happens."

"We wouldn't want that," Clint had replied, standing up, "would we?"

"No," Cartwright said, "we wouldn't."

So Clint slept and knew he'd awaken early. With the morning sun he'd go out and have a look at Philadelphia—and let whoever this informer was take a good look at him.

A good long look.

Bob Lester waited over an hour and was just about to give up when the man finally arrived at their prearranged meeting place.

"I just about gave up on you," Les said to the man.

"I told you I'd be here," the man said. "Did you do it?"

"I sure did," Les said. "I just left my cab outside the station, and he came right to me."

"And where did you take him?"

"Right where I said I would," Les said. "The Holiday Hotel."

"Stupid name for a hotel," the man said.

"Nice place, though."

"If you say so."

"What about my money?"

"Oh yeah," the man said. "Your money. Sure. Here it is."

The man took out a gun, and Les's eyes widened. He didn't have a chance to cry out before the gun sounded once. The bullet struck him in the chest and went right to his heart. He was dead before his body hit the ground.

The other man took a moment to check and make sure that Les was dead, then turned and walked away.

FOUR

A knock on the door woke Clint, who sat up in bed and stared at the window accusingly. The morning sun was supposed to have awakened him, but there was no sun coming in. That's because it was overcast outside. As he stared at the window a sheet of rain suddenly struck it, and probably would have awakened him, if he hadn't been awake already.

The pounding on the door sounded again, reminding him of what it was that had actually awakened him.

"All right," he called out irritably, "I'm coming."

He felt oddly angry at the sun for not coming out. It was as if that big ball of light had betrayed him. He pulled on his trousers and went to answer the door.

"Mr. Adams?"

Clint stared at the uniformed Philadelphia police officer and frowned.

"Are you Mr. Clint Adams?" the officer asked.

"That's right," Clint said, wondering if this fresh-faced young policeman could be his informer. "Can I do something for you?"

"Yes, sir, you can," the policeman said. "You can come with me."

"Come with you? Where?"

"My superior would like to talk to you."

"Your superior?"

"Yes, sir," the man said. "That would be Lieutenant Kelly."

"Kelly," Clint said. Could this Lieutenant Kelly be the informer, and if he was, would he send another policeman to get him? Perhaps he was going to make the contact under the guise of questioning him.

"What's this about . . ."

"Willis."

"What?"

"That's me," the man said. "Officer Willis."

"Can you tell me what this is all about, Officer Willis?" Clint asked.

"I really can't, sir. I'm sorry."

"Well . . . it is rather early, isn't it, Officer Willis?"

"I know it is, sir, and I'm sorry about waking you so early," Willis said, "but Lieutenant Kelly told me to bring you right back with me." The man sincerely looked as if he regretted having to wake him.

"Back where?"

"Police headquarters, sir."

"Do I have time to get dressed?" Clint asked.

"Oh, of course, sir," the policeman answered, as if it were a serious question. "I'll wait for you down in the lobby."

"I'll be down in a few minutes," Clint promised. "Just let me wash up and get dressed."

"Of course, sir."

Clint wondered if the young policeman's manners could possibly be on the level. Was anyone that polite?

He closed the door, thoughtfully poured some water from the pitcher on the dresser into a basin, and washed his hands and face. After that he dressed and decided that whatever this was about, it probably had nothing to do with the informer. If the man wanted to observe him before contacting him, he certainly hadn't had ample time to do that. This summons to police headquarters had to be about something else entirely—although he had no idea what it could be. He'd only been in the city a matter of hours. What kind of trouble could he have gotten into? Or had he been recognized?

Well, he'd find that all out soon enough.

He reached for his gun belt and then thought better of it. It wouldn't do to go to police headquarters wearing his regular Colt. Instead he took the little Colt New Line out of his carpetbag and tucked it into his belt at the small of his back. It would be visible, but not as obvious as the holster.

He left the room and went down to the lobby.

Officer Willis was waiting, as promised. Clint looked over at the desk and saw that Harold was on duty behind it. The desk clerk gave him a quick glance, and then just as quickly looked away. There was an air of guilt about him. Had Harold recognized him the day before and notified the police? Harold Lester was certainly feeling guilty about something. Clint wondered what it was.

"Ready, sir?" Willis asked.

"Yes, I'm ready, Officer Willis."

"I have a carriage waiting outside, sir. Thank you for being so prompt."

"Thank you for being so polite," Clint said.

"Oh, it's nothing, sir," Willis said. "This way, please."

Clint followed him outside. . . .

Across the street from the hotel, from the sanctuary of a doorway, a man watched as Clint and the police officer left the hotel and climbed into a carriage. The man scratched his head and ran his hand down over his face as the carriage pulled away. When it was out of sight, he nervously tugged at his clothes and stepped from the doorway, looking both ways, then started across the street.

FIVE

Police headquarters turned out to be a fairly modern-looking brick structure about three stories high. The carriage stopped directly in front, and Clint followed Willis up the stairs and into the building.

"We won't have to stop at the front desk," Willis said. "The lieutenant will be waiting in his office."

"Fine."

He followed Willis past the front desk, watching as the young man exchanged a nod with the older sergeant. They went down a hallway until they reached a closed door, which Willis knocked on.

"Come in," a man's voice called out.

Willis opened the door and allowed Clint to go in ahead of him.

"Mr. Adams, sir."

"Thank you, Willis. You can go."

"Yes, sir," Willis said, closing the door as he withdrew.

"Mr. Adams," said the man behind the desk. "Have a seat, please."

Clint moved forward and sat in the chair opposite the desk. The man behind it was about his own age. He had brown hair streaked with gray and a carefully groomed mustache which had the same streaking.

"He's a polite young man," Clint said.

"Willis?" Kelly said. "Yes, but he'll get over it. I'm Lieutenant Kenneth Kelly." The lieutenant rose and gave Clint a short handshake, then sat back down.

"Lieutenant, can you tell me why I was brought here so early in the morning?"

"Well, the hour hardly matters, does it, Mr. Adams?" Kelly said. "I mean, even if we had brought you here in the afternoon, or the evening, you'd still want to know why, wouldn't you?"

Clint stared at the man without answering, wondering if the man was deliberately trying to get a rise out of him.

"In any case," Kelly said, setting his hands on his desk and clasping them together, "you want to know why you're here. It seems we had a murder last night. We were wondering if you'd be able to help us with it."

Clint decided to play it as obtuse as the lieutenant himself was playing it.

"Are you under the impression that I'm a detective, Lieutenant?"

Kelly's mustache twitched and he said, "No, I am not, sir. It happens you were one of the last people to see the victim alive."

"I don't know how that can be," Clint said. "I only arrived last night, and I only came into contact with three people, the desk clerk, the driver who brought me to the hotel from the train station, and the waitress who served me dinner. Now, unless one of them was murdered—"

"One of them was," Kelly said, cutting him off.

Clint frowned. He had already seen the desk clerk alive, so that left the driver, or the waitress.

"Which one?" he asked.

"The driver," Kelly said. "His name was . . . Robert Lester."

"Les," Clint said.

"Yes," Kelly said, "I believe that was what he was called."

"How was he killed?"

"He was shot," Kelly said. "His body was found in a deserted part of the city."

"I don't know what I can tell you," Clint said. "All he did was drive me to the hotel."

"We know that."

"Who told you?"

"The desk clerk."

"The cousin?"

"I beg your pardon?"

"Was his name Harold? The desk clerk?"

"I believe so, yes. What was that you said . . . about a cousin?"

"Harold and Les, they were cousins."

Kelly frowned.

"He didn't tell you that?"

"No," Kelly said. "He neglected to mention it."

"He mentioned me, though."

"Yes."

"Well, I can't help you, Lieutenant," Clint said. "I didn't see Les again after he left me at the hotel."

"Did he speak to anyone else at the station? Someone you might have noticed?"

"No," Clint said. "He was dozing. I woke him and asked to be taken to a hotel. We went directly from the station to my hotel. He didn't speak to anyone, not even after we arrived."

"I see."

"That's all I can tell you."

"I see," Kelly said again. "Well, thank you for coming in. I appreciate your cooperation. You can go. I'm sorry if we've inconvenienced you."

Clint stood up.

"No inconvenience, Lieutenant," he said. "I wish I could have been more helpful."

"Yes," Kelly said, "so do I."

Clint started for the door, then stopped and turned around.

"You'll be questioning the cousin again, won't you?" he asked.

"Oh, yes," Kelly said. "You can bet on that."

"He didn't seem to like his cousin much," Clint said. "For what that's worth. He called him the black sheep of the family."

Kelly digested that piece of information and then said, "Thanks."

"Glad to help," Clint said, and left the office.

He retraced his steps back to the front desk, where the sergeant eyed him suspiciously. Officer Willis was there also, talking to the man behind the desk.

"All finished?" Willis asked.

"Yes," Clint said. "How do I get back to my hotel?"

"Oh, I'll take you, sir," Willis said. "It's the least I can do after waking you so early."

Willis headed for the front door, and Clint looked

at the desk sergeant once again. This time the man wasn't looking at him suspiciously. He was looking at him as if to say, "Do you believe him?"

Clint shrugged and followed Willis outside.

SIX

When Clint returned to his hotel he walked directly to the front desk. Harold had his head down and didn't see him coming until he was almost upon him. When the clerk did notice him, his eyes went wide and he started looking around, either for someone to help him, or for somewhere to run.

"I heard your black sheep cousin got killed last night," Clint said.

"Uh . . . that's right, that's what I heard," Harold said nervously.

"I'll bet you were all upset when you heard, huh?" Clint asked.

"Well . . . of course. After all, he *was* my cousin," Harold said.

"But not too upset to give them my name, right?"

"Uh . . ."

"I mean, all I did was get a ride to the hotel with him, but you thought that was enough of a reason to give the police my name, right?"

"Well . . ."

24

"Or maybe you just wanted to make sure they didn't question *you* about the murder."

"Me?" Harold said, surprised. "Why should they question me?"

"I'll bet you didn't tell them he was your cousin, did you?"

"Well, I . . ."

"Your black sheep cousin, right? The one who brought disgrace to the family name?"

"I never said—"

"Well, don't worry, Harold," Clint said, "*I* told them he was your cousin."

"What ?"

"I told them how you felt about him."

"What did you—"

"They'll probably be here any minute to talk to you," Clint said. "Make sure you tell them everything they want to know. They don't take kindly to being lied to."

"But I didn't—"

"Oh, by the way, do I have any messages?"

"Messages? Uh, no, no messages. Listen, uh, what did you tell—"

"Have a good day."

Clint left the clerk sputtering and went up to his room. Inside he sat on the bed and shook his head in disbelief. Barely in town and already he had been to see the police. How did he get himself into these messes? Doing favors for Jim West and the United States government, that's how.

He stripped off the clothes he had worn yesterday, washed up and donned fresh clothes, then went downstairs to have breakfast.

SEVEN

During breakfast Clint talked at length with the pretty waitress. Specifically, he was wondering what there was to do in Philadelphia.

"I guess that depends on what you like to do," she said. "Uh, what *do* you like to do?"

"Oh, the usual," Clint said, thinking of poker and beer.

"The theater? Museums?" she asked.

"Is that what you like to do?" he asked.

"Oh, yes," she said. "I love the theater. There's a wonderful production of *Hamlet* in town now. Do you know *Hamlet*?"

"Shakespeare, right?" Clint asked.

"That's right," she said, pleased. "Have you seen it?"

"Uh, no, I haven't."

"I have," she said. "Twice so far. In fact, I was thinking of going again tonight."

"Really?"

"I just hate to go alone," she said, and then stood there expectantly.

Never one to disappoint a lady, Clint said, "Well, I have nothing to do tonight. Would you like me to go with you?"

"That would be great," she said. "I have to go home at five and change."

"Tell me where you live and—"

"Oh, no," she said, cutting him off. "I'll meet you back here. The theater isn't far from here. We could walk."

"All right, Alison," he said. She looked even more pleased that he had remembered her name. "What time should I meet you?"

"Meet me out front at seven," she said. "It's Clint, right?"

"Yes, that's right."

"I asked at the desk," she said, a bit sheepishly.

"I'm glad you did," he said. He stood up and reached into his pocket to tip her.

"No, that's all right," she said. "It's enough that you're going to the theater with me. I really hate to go alone."

"Who did you go with the other two times?"

"I went alone," she said.

A question occurred to him, and he asked it.

"Do you have a boyfriend?"

"I do . . . well, I *did*," she said. "I'm not seeing him anymore."

"He wouldn't go to the theater with you?"

"Among other things," she said. "He just wasn't . . . what I thought he was."

"How long did you know him?"

"All my life," she said. "He's older than me, but

I've known him since I was a baby."

"That long, huh?"

"But we're not seeing each other anymore," she said again.

"I see," Clint said. "Well then, I'll see you at seven."

"What will you do with the rest of the day?" she asked as he was about to leave.

"Oh, I don't know," he said. "Walk around the city, I guess. Maybe I'll just go and take a look at the Liberty Bell."

"Wait for me."

"What?"

"Wait for me to see the Liberty Bell. I'll take you over there."

"All right," he said. "I'll walk around, but I won't look at the Liberty Bell."

"See you at seven," she said as he left, and then stood there watching him, her arms folded, as he walked out into the lobby.

In the lobby Clint saw Police Officer Willis standing off to one side, and then noticed Lieutenant Kelly talking to Harold at the desk. Clint walked over to join Willis.

"How come the lieutenant comes here to talk to him, but he had me brought to his office?" Clint asked.

"I really don't know why the lieutenant does the things he does," Willis said, "but I'm watching him closely."

"Really?"

"Oh yes," Willis said sincerely. "I'm learning from him every day."

"I see," Clint said. "Willis, were you always this . . . sincere?"

Willis took his eyes off of the lieutenant to look at Clint.

"Sincere, sir?"

"Well, you're very polite and sincere," Clint said. "Hasn't anyone ever pointed that out to you before?"

"No, sir," Willis said thoughtfully. "Thank you for pointing it out. I try to be as polite and truthful as I can be, but sincere? Yes, I'm very pleased that you pointed that out to me."

"Did you go to college, Officer Willis?"

"Oh, of course," Willis said. "I felt it was my duty to get a good education, so I'd be able to support my family."

"And so you became a policeman?"

Willis smiled, a patient, tolerant smile and said, "This is just a stepping-stone to bigger and better things, sir."

"Ah," Clint said. "Politics?"

"Yes, sir."

"I see," Clint said. "You'll be moving to Washington, then."

"Yes, sir," Willis said, "but that's a long way off. First I have to learn all I can from the lieutenant and then . . ."

"And then move on to someone else and learn from them," Clint said.

"Exactly."

"You're an interesting young man, Officer Willis," Clint said.

"Why, thank you."

Clint had never heard a man so politely explain

how he would be using other people to get where he wanted to go in his life.

"Interesting," Clint said again. "Have a good day."

"You too, sir."

Clint looked over to where Kelly was still questioning Harold. The clerk tossed him a worried look over the lieutenant's shoulder, and Kelly turned and looked at him. If he recognized Clint he gave no indication. He simply turned his head and went back to questioning the desk clerk.

EIGHT

Clint walked around in the immediate area for a while. He wasn't looking for anything in particular as much as he was affording someone the chance to look *him* over.

He had to assume that whoever the informer was had to have been watching the train station for him. The man—if it was a man—wouldn't have known what hotel Clint would register in, although the 36th Street Station had been specified as the one Clint should get off at. Still, Les had taken him a long way from the station for a hotel. The only way for the informant to know that Clint had arrived was for him to have been watching that station. That meant that he had probably followed Les's cab from the station, and now knew what hotel Clint was staying at.

With all of that thinking out of the way he decided that all he needed to do was parade himself around in the area near the hotel to give the informer a chance to look him over.

It was a little after noon when he found himself passing a saloon that was open for business. He decided to stop in for an afternoon beer.

The place was small and clean, with several tables and a polished bar. There was no one else there at the moment, except for the bartender, a tall man with long arms and knobby knuckles who was wiping down the already shining bar top.

"First customer of the day," the man said. "What can I get you?"

"A beer."

The bartender drew the beer and set it down in front of him.

"You here from out West?" the man asked.

"That's right," Clint said. "How did you know?"

"The gun," the man said, and Clint looked down at the gun on his hip. "Most fellas from the West still wear it when they walk around. This is the city, fella, not the wild West. You don't need that thing."

"You're probably right," Clint said. He'd start leaving the gun in the hotel and carry the New Line, instead. It would never occur to him to walk around totally without a gun.

"What brings you to Philadelphia?" the man asked.

"Just taking a look around," Clint said.

"Looking to settle in the East?"

Clint sipped his cold beer and said, "I'm not looking to settle anywhere."

The bartender leaned his elbows on the bar and looked intently at Clint.

"I got a wife and three kids," he said. "There ain't nothin' like it, friend. A home, a family, a good woman—of course, you probably have no problems in that department."

"What department?"

"Women," the man said. "You look like a fella who can handle himself when it comes to women."

"I get by."

"See?" the man said. "See what I mean?"

"About what?"

"Most men, they talk and talk about all the women they have, it means they ain't got any. They're just talkin'. Now, the men who do okay with the women? They don't talk about it at all, like you. They have all the reason in the world to brag, and they don't." The man shook his head and said, "People, I love 'em."

"In this business you see a lot of them."

"You bet I do," the man said. "All kinds, too."

"Did you know a cab driver named Robert Lester?"

"Les?" the man said. "Sure, I knew him. What a crime, huh?" He shook his head. "Somebody shootin' him like that. Les was all right. He always had a little somethin' goin', but he was all right."

"What do you mean, a little somethin'?" Clint asked, frowning. He put his beer mug down on the bar, still half full.

"You want another one?"

"I'll finish this one," Clint said. "What did you mean about a little somethin'?"

"You know, an angle, somethin' goin' on the side," the man said.

"You mean something illegal?"

"Well," the man said, lowering his voice, "if a fella like Les wanted to make a few bucks, he wouldn't do it on somethin' *legal* . . . if you get my meaning."

"I think I do," Clint said.

"Did you know Les?"

"He picked me up at the station and took me to my hotel," Clint said. He touched his mug, made little wet circles on the bar with it. When he looked up the bartender was looking down at the circles.

"Oh, sorry," Clint said.

"That's okay," the man said. "It wipes off, huh? Like this." He swiped at the bar once with his rag, and the circles were gone. "That's how I keep it so shiny, you know?"

"You own this place?"

"Yep, it's all mine," the man said. He put the rag down, wiped his palm on the side of his pants, and extended his hand. "Dennis Collins. Hi."

Clint shook the man's hand and said, "Clint Adams. Glad to meet you."

"You, uh, didn't have anything going with Les, did you, Clint?"

"Anything going?"

"I mean, he wasn't gettin' you anythin', was he? 'Cause if he was, and you're still interested, I might be able to help you—if you know what I mean."

"Yeah," Clint said, "I know what you mean, and no, I didn't have anything going with him."

"Well, if you change your mind and you—ya know, want somethin'? Keep me in mind."

"I'll do that," Clint said. He finished his beer, put the empty mug down, and dropped some money on the bar.

"That's too much," Dennis said.

"It's enough," Clint said.

"Thanks."

"Thanks for the beer," Clint said. "And the offer."

"You come back," Collins said. "This is a small place, and it usually stays quiet. You wanna drink someplace quiet, you come to Denny's Saloon, okay?"

"I'll remember."

Clint stepped outside, where it was overcast and threatening to rain again. He hoped it held off until he got back to his hotel.

NINE

When Clint saw Police Officer Willis in the lobby of the hotel, he suddenly had the feeling that someone was playing him for a fool. Willis was there either to watch Harold, Les's cousin, or to watch Clint. Either way, Kelly wouldn't entrust a portion of a murder investigation to someone of Willis's obvious inexperience. That could only mean that Willis wasn't as inexperienced, or naive, as he made himself out to be.

Either that, or Clint didn't know what the hell he was talking about.

"Hello, Officer Willis," he said, greeting the young man.

"Mr. Adams," Willis said. "How was your walk?"

"It was very nice."

"Did you see the Liberty Bell?"

"No, I didn't get a chance to see the Liberty Bell yet," Clint said.

"You should," Willis said. "It's very impressive—inspiring."

"I'm looking forward to it, Willis. Tell me something, will you?"

"If I can."

"What are you doing here?"

"Working."

"I assumed that," Clint said. "Are you watching me?"

Willis frowned.

"Why would I be watching you, sir?"

"Oh, I don't know," Clint said. "I'm a stranger in your city, and there's been a murder."

"Just because you're a stranger doesn't make you a suspect," Willis said.

"That's how I feel," Clint said. "I wonder if Lieutenant Kelly feels the same way."

"I don't know, sir," Willis said, looking and sounding *so* sincere.

"Willis . . ."

"Yes, sir?"

Clint was going to ask him if he was actually that sincere, then decided against it.

"Never mind. . . . Keep up the good work."

"Yes, sir," Willis said. "I will, sir."

Maybe he was imagining things. Maybe there were still people like Willis in the world. Maybe Clint Adams was just too damned cynical for his own good.

He meant to spend the rest of the afternoon in his room, but after an hour of that he became too impatient. He went back downstairs to the lobby. He was pleased not only to see that Willis was gone, but that Harold was not the clerk on the desk. He exchanged a friendly nod with the clerk who was there and walked to the front door.

He stepped outside and looked around. There were people walking by on both sides of the street, but there didn't seem to be anyone standing around specifically watching the building.

The hotel had a small porch with some chairs on it, and he decided to occupy one of the chairs for a while and watch the city go by. He had left his holster in his room and had the New Line stuck into the back of his belt. When he sat down, it pressed comfortably into the small of his back.

From a window across the street, a man watched as Clint sat down and leaned back, seemingly content to sit and watch as people walked by. Well, the man was content to stay where he was and watch Clint Adams—for a while, anyway.

TEN

Clint had been sitting in front of the hotel for about an hour when Lieutenant Kelly appeared. As Kelly approached the porch, Clint realized that he wasn't surprised to see the man.

"Good afternoon," Kelly said.

"Lieutenant."

"Mind if I sit?"

Clint made a gesture with his hand to the chair next to him, and Kelly sat in it.

"Taking it easy, are you?"

"That's right," Clint said. He pointed and said, "I'm watching your city go by."

"How do you like it, so far?"

"So far it's nice, and quiet."

"Except for murder."

Clint looked at Kelly and said, "Yes, except for that. Is this is a coincidence, Lieutenant, or did you come here specifically to talk to me?"

"Well . . . naturally I came to talk to you, Mr. Adams," Kelly said. "This morning, when we spoke,

I didn't know who you were."

"I told you who I was," Clint said.

"You told me your name," Kelly said. "I mean *who* you were . . . your reputation."

"Oh," Clint said, turning his head, "that."

"Yes, that. What brings a celebrated Western gunman to my city, Mr. Adams?"

Clint looked at Kelly and said, "The way you're thinking now? That's what brought me here."

"I don't—"

"Understand? I came here to get away from people who know who I am," Clint explained.

"I see," Kelly said. "You don't care for your reputation?"

"Reputations are like egos," Clint said.

"I beg your pardon?"

"Inflated," Clint said, "and usually for the wrong reasons."

"I see," Kelly said again. "That's a very good analogy."

"Thank you."

"Tell me," Kelly said, "do you carry a gun?"

"Of course," Clint said.

"I see you're not wearing your holster," Kelly said. "Is it in your room?"

"Yes."

"Do you have a gun on you at the moment?"

"Yes, I do," Clint said.

"May I see it?"

Clint leaned forward, withdrew the gun from the back of his belt, and handed it to the lieutenant, butt first. The man took it, examined it, checked to see if it was fully loaded and if it had been recently fired, and then returned it. Clint tucked the gun in his belt once more and leaned back in his seat again.

"Did you have that on you when you came to see me this morning?"

Clint debated lying, then decided against it.

"Yes, I did."

"I'd like to see your other gun, if you have no objection," Kelly said.

"I have no objection, Lieutenant," Clint said. "Would you like to see it right now?"

Lieutenant Kelly smiled and said, "If it's not too inconvenient."

Clint smiled back and said, "Now why would it be inconvenient, Lieutenant? All you have to do is come upstairs with me—that is, unless you'd rather I brought it down?"

"No," Kelly said, standing, "that's all right. *That* would be inconvenient. You'd only have to take it back upstairs again. I'll come up with you and take a look at it."

Sure, Clint thought, and take a look at my room at the same time.

ELEVEN

Clint unlocked the door and entered the room ahead of Lieutenant Kelly. He stepped aside to allow Kelly to come in, then closed the door behind them. It was odd. He knew there was nothing incriminating in the room but still found himself looking around to be sure.

"The gun belt is there," he said, pointing, "on the bedpost."

Kelly walked to the holster, removed the gun, checked the loads and if it had been fired recently. He also hefted the gun, getting the feel of it.

"Nice weapon."

"Thanks."

"You do work on it yourself?"

"That's right."

"This gun has been cleaned recently," Kelly said, replacing it.

"Not really," Clint said. "I like to keep my weapon in working order. Let's just say that it's been cleaned more recently than it's been fired."

Kelly nodded and said, "Fair enough."

He stood where he was for a moment, looking around the room. It wasn't much more than a glance, but Clint knew that the man was taking everything in—not that there was anything to take in.

"Is there a problem?"

"No," Kelly said, "no problem. I was just wondering why a man like yourself would be staying here instead of one of the more expensive hotels."

"What do you mean, a man like myself? Are you under the impression that I'm a man of wealth?"

"Well, you *are* a man of some notoriety," Kelly said.

"That doesn't translate into dollars and cents, Lieutenant."

"Forgive me," Kelly said. "I'm not at all sure how to act around a living legend."

Clint frowned, but remained silent. He had the feeling the policeman was trying to get a rise out of him. He wasn't going to give the man the satisfaction.

"Have you seen enough?" he asked.

"Quite enough, thank you," Kelly said. "Shall we go back downstairs?"

"I have to take a bath and get ready to go out," Clint said.

"Ah, a night on the town?" Kelly asked.

"I'm going to the theater."

"To see what?"

"*Hamlet.*"

"Shakespeare," Kelly said. "I've seen it many times. I'm afraid this performance doesn't quite do it justice."

"The words are still there," Clint said.

"That's true," Kelly said.

He walked to the door, put his hand on the knob, then turned around.

"You don't strike me as the Shakespeare type," he said frankly.

"I'm not," Clint said truthfully. "I'm escorting a lady."

Kelly smiled.

"Not even in town twenty-four hours and you're escorting a lady to the theater already? Perhaps your notoriety is not worth money, but there are other advantages, aren't—"

"Lieutenant," Clint said, "I really do have to get to that bath."

"Of course," Kelly said. "Enjoy the play."

"Thank you."

Kelly opened the door, then turned back to Clint once again.

"Mr. Adams, would you be able to give me some idea of how long you'll be in Philadelphia?"

"I'm not sure that I can, Lieutenant."

Kelly smiled patiently and said, "A rough estimate, then?"

"Several days, perhaps."

"Perhaps longer . . . or shorter?"

"Longer, perhaps," Clint conceded. "Certainly no shorter."

"I see," Kelly said. "Well, thank you for your cooperation. Again, enjoy the play."

As Kelly left, it occurred to Clint that the man had been exceedingly polite. It looked as if Officer Willis really was observing the good lieutenant's methods quite closely.

• • •

The man in the window across the street had recognized Lieutenant Kenneth Kelly as soon as he arrived. He watched with interest as Kelly and Clint Adams conversed, and then both men rose and went into the hotel. About fifteen minutes later Lieutenant Kelly came out by himself. The man watched the lieutenant walk away from the hotel until he was out of sight. He watched the front of the hotel intently, waiting to see if Clint Adams would come out again. When he didn't, the man assumed that Adams would be inside for a while.

Rather than moving away from the window, the man lit a long, thin, dark cigar and settled in to wait for the Gunsmith's reappearance.

TWELVE

Clint came out of the hotel at about ten to seven and reclaimed his chair. He was freshly bathed and wearing the best clothes he had brought with him. He hadn't planned on attending the theater, but he thought this suit of clothes would pass muster. He usually travelled with some sort of a suit when he was going to a city like New York, San Francisco . . . or Philadelphia.

He sat back, getting comfortable, enjoying the feel of the little gun in the small of his back. His jacket would hide it from view tonight, but would not keep him from getting at it in a hurry, if the need arose.

He waited about twenty minutes before a hansom cab pulled by two horses arrived in front of the hotel. It was a much better cab than the one he had taken to the hotel from the station, with Les. He watched as a man dropped down from the driver's seat and opened the back door. Alison stepped out, with the driver's assistance, dressed in a lovely gown that was either purple or lavender. Clint wasn't sure what the difference was, but it looked like an expensive gown.

She stood there, smiling at him, and he rose and walked down to the carriage, where she was waiting.

"You look beautiful," he said, and meant it. At work she was pretty, but dressed like this, and wearing makeup, she looked nothing short of beautiful.

"Thank you. Shall we go?"

The driver opened the door again, and Clint helped Alison climb in, then got in after her. The rig was very fancy, and Clint wondered if Alison was paying for it herself out of her waitress salary.

"This is pretty fancy," he said, giving voice to his thoughts.

"I thought it would be nice to go to the theater in style," she said.

"Nice, and expensive," he said.

"Don't worry about that, Clint," she said. "Everything is taken care of."

He wondered what she meant by *everything*.

The observer from the window across the street found the proceedings very interesting. He watched as the cab stopped in front of the hotel and then a young woman got out. It seemed that Clint Adams had not wasted any time finding himself some female companionship—and this was no whore. At least, she wasn't a *cheap* whore.

The man left the window and ran downstairs before the cab could pull away out of sight.

From a room inside the hotel another man was looking out a window. He saw everything the first

man saw, and then he saw the first man come out
of the building across the street and hurry after the
hansom cab. The man was probably either going to
try to follow on foot—which wouldn't be difficult,
since the cabs didn't move particularly fast—or he'd
hail his own cab somewhere along the way.

This second man made no move to follow, as he
already knew where Clint Adams and the young lady
were going. He took his time going downstairs. He
would find his own cab at his leisure and arrive at
the theater in plenty of time.

"Okay, I have to ask," Clint said finally, "and
before we get to the theater."

"I know," Alison said sheepishly. "What's a waitress doing in a cab like this, wearing a gown like
this? Is that right?"

"You're a mind reader."

"Not really," she said. "I hope this won't shock
you, Clint, or scare you away."

"What?"

She hesitated, then blurted it out as if it was some
terrible sin.

"My father is rich."

"Is that all?" he said. "I thought you had some
terrible, dark secret."

"That *is* my secret," she said. "Nobody at the hotel
knows. They think I'm just a waitress."

"Well, why *are* you a waitress?"

"Because it's good, honest work," she said, "and
I need to be doing honest work. I can't live by my
father's money." She looked sheepish again as she
realized where they were and what she was wearing
and added, "Well, not totally, anyway."

"What have you got against money?"

"Nothing," she said, "but it's not *my* money, it's my father's. He bought me the gown, and he has tickets to the theater for every performance, no matter what's playing. I love the theater."

Clint thought he understood. She did enjoy her father's money to some degree, but in order not to feel guilty about it, she had to work at her own job. Well, he didn't see anything wrong with any of that. It meant that she had character.

"Well," he said, "I'm not shocked, and I'm not scared away."

She smiled and said, "That's good, that's very good. We're going to have a good time tonight."

Clint wondered what she meant by a good time.

THIRTEEN

Alison's company was fine, the play was brilliant, but Lieutenant Kelly had been right about the performance. The actors weren't quite up to the material, but even Clint—who had never seen *Hamlet* before—recognized the genius in the author.

As they were filing out of the theater with the crowd, Alison asked, "Well, what did you think of it?"

"I thought the play was wonderful," he said.

"Did you enjoy it?"

"Thoroughly."

"Even with the bad acting?" she asked, as if it was her fault the performances were bad.

"It just makes me want to see it again, but with good acting."

"Oh, I'm glad," she said, clapping her hands together like a little girl. "I'm always glad when I can interest someone in the theater."

"Well, I've been to the theater before," he said, not bothering to mention that he had once been *in* the theater for a very short time. "I had just never seen Shakespeare before."

"Oh, and there's so much more," she said. "There's *Romeo and Juliet*, *Macbeth*, *A Midsummer Night's Dream*—"

"They're not *all* playing here in Philadelphia, are they?" he asked, cutting her off.

"No, of course not," she said. "I just want you to know about them so you can go and see them when they are playing someplace near you."

"I appreciate the fact that you're trying to give me culture, Alison," Clint said. "Should we go someplace to eat now?"

"I know a nice place," she said.

"Is it expensive?"

She nodded, her eyes shining, and said, "*And* it's decadent."

"Then by all means," he said, "let's go."

Outside the theater they headed for the rented hansom cab. As they were approaching it, Clint saw a man coming toward them from their right.

"Alison, this boyfriend of yours?"

"He *used* to be my boyfriend."

"Right. . . . What's he looks like?"

She saw where he was looking and turned her head. He heard her groan.

"He looks like that!" she said.

The man was in his early thirties, and he was a strapping six four if he was an inch, with wide shoulders and bulging biceps that strained the fabric of his shirt. He had very black hair, and his two eyebrows looked like one that went straight across his forehead.

"Who's this guy?" the man demanded.

"Arthur," she said, "what are you doing here?"

"I know what you like, Alison," he said. "I knew you'd be here. I wanted to see who you'd be here with."

He stuck his jaw out and glared at Clint, who knew that if he needed one, that jaw made an inviting target. The big man made a very improbable "Arthur."

"Who's this guy?"

"None of your business," she said. "He's my escort for the evening."

"Oh, is that so?" Arthur said. He looked at Clint and said, "This is *my* girl you're *escorting*, mister. Did you know that?"

"I know she *used* to be your girl," Clint said.

"Used to be?" Arthur said, frowning. "Who told you that?"

"She did."

"Ha!" The man laughed. "She don't make those decisions, friend; I do."

"Is that so?" Alison demanded. She put both her hands against the man's massive chest and pushed, barely budging him. "Well, I'm telling you now, Arthur, I am not your girl. Stop making a scene here."

She glanced around at the small crowd of onlookers they had attracted.

"I ain't makin' a scene, Alison," Arthur said. "You are."

"Arthur," she said, "we can talk about this another time. Right now I want you to go."

"Alison—"

"Go, Arthur . . . now!"

Arthur chose that moment to glare at Clint again, anvil jaw jutting out.

"Mister," Arthur said, "this ain't over."

"It hasn't even begun," Clint said.

"We'll see," Arthur said.

"Come on, Clint," Alison said. "Let's get in the carriage."

As Clint helped her into the carriage and climbed in behind her, Arthur shouted, "What's your father gonna think of this, Alison?"

Alison stuck her head out the window and shouted, "He doesn't make my decisions for me any more than you do, Arthur! Driver—go!"

FOURTEEN

As the carriage pulled away from the theater Alison leaned her head back and closed her eyes, remaining like that for a few moments. Clint left her alone, deciding that she was either catching her breath, collecting her thoughts, or both.

"I'm sorry," she finally said. "I had no idea he'd be there, I really didn't."

"That's all right," Clint said.

"He's insufferable," she said. "He's just like my father. They both think they can run my life."

"Alison . . . who is your father? I assume, if he's wealthy, that he's probably fairly well-known."

"Only if you're from Philadelphia . . . or from the East. His name is Orville Becker."

"What's his business?"

"He builds ships."

"Ships?"

"Yes . . . boats, ships, whatever they're called."

"Who does he build them for?" Clint asked.

"Oh, for anyone with enough money to pay him,

but he does a lot of work for the government."

"The United States government?" Clint asked.

"Well . . . yes, of course. What other government would he be working for?"

"I'm sorry," Clint said. "I was just . . . surprised."

"That doesn't scare you, does it?" Alison asked. "That Daddy works with the government?"

"No, why should it scare me?"

"I don't know," she said. "It scares a lot of men. How about Arthur?"

"What about him?"

"Did he scare you?"

"Well, I was impressed by his size," Clint said, "but I'm not scared of him."

"That's good," she said.

"I take it, from what I heard Arthur say, that your father approves of him?"

"Daddy is crazy about Arthur—as husband material, I mean. He just about promised me to Arthur and his family when I was younger. The two of them think that if they scare off every other man, I'll *have* to marry Arthur. I'm glad you're not scared."

Uh-oh, Clint thought.

"Alison, I'm not afraid, but I'm not husband material, either."

She laughed and put her hand on his arm.

"Oh, I didn't mean that you were," Alison said. "I'm just glad to find a man who isn't frightened of them. It gives me hope that there are more out there."

"I take it you don't want to marry Arthur?" Clint asked.

"I don't want to marry any man who wants to run me, Clint. I have a mind of my own. That's why I work."

"I admire you for that," he said.

"You do?"

"Yes, I do."

She leaned over and kissed his cheek. Her lips were soft, and her scent lingered in his nose.

"We'll be at the restaurant shortly," she said, and put her head on his shoulder.

Clint was grateful for the respite in the conversation. He was thinking about Alison's father working for the government. His assignment here involved the government, and to find out that her father was involved with them was—well, he just didn't like coincidences. In the morning he was going to have to send a telegram to Washington to run a check on Mr. Orville Becker, the shipbuilder.

When they arrived at the restaurant Clint was impressed. It looked more like some sort of a hall, where great parties or balls would be held. Inside it was all leather, oak, and crystal chandeliers.

A man in a tuxedo greeted Alison by name—"Miss Alison"—and showed them to a table. Another man in a white tuxedo came to take their order, and also addressed Alison as "Miss" Alison. The maître d' had even gone so far as to inquire about her father's health.

"He's fine, Andrew, just fine," she had said.

"Please send him my regards," Andrew said. "Tell him we miss seeing him here."

"I'll tell him."

In the time it took Andrew to walk away and the waiter to walk over she leaned across the table and said to Clint, "They miss Daddy's *money*."

"I can see why," he said. "This place must cost a fortune to run."

When the waiter came, Alison asked Clint, "May I order for both of us?"

Remembering what she'd said about men trying to run her life, he said, "Go ahead, Alison. The night is yours."

She ordered pheasant for the two of them, with green vegetables prepared with almonds, french bread, and a bottle of wine.

"I should have ordered champagne," she said when the waiter left.

"Are we celebrating something?" Clint asked.

"Well, I haven't told anyone," she said, and then added, "and no one's remembered."

"What?"

"Today's my birthday," she said. "I'm twenty-four today."

"Happy birthday!" he said. "I wish I had known, I would have bought you something."

"I purposely didn't tell you," she said. "I just wanted to go to the theater, and to dinner, and I wanted to go with someone who . . . who wouldn't try to tell me what to do every step of the way. That's enough of a birthday gift, believe me. Except for those few moments with Arthur, I'm having a wonderful time."

"I'm glad," Clint said.

He would have been having a nice time, too, if he wasn't still thinking about her father and the United States government. Hearing that had colored the way he was looking at her. It was even possible that *she* was the informant.

What if it was her *father* who was plotting something, and *she* wanted to turn him in? He couldn't very well come right out and ask her about it . . . could he?

As the hansom cab left the theater area, Arthur Pinkney stared hard after it. If his first name was ill-fitting, that went double for his last name. Still, no one had ever made fun of Arthur's name while he was growing up—at least, they hadn't made fun of it *twice*.

He was going to teach this new fellow of Alison's a lesson, too, just like he used to do to the kids in school. Yep, this new fellow of hers wouldn't be going out with her again. He'd done it once, but he wasn't about to do it twice. Arthur Pinkney would see to that.

A lot of people had witnessed the altercation between Clint Adams, Alison Becker, and Arthur Pinkney, but two people in particular had taken keen interest.

They didn't know each other, these two unseen observers, but they were thinking the same thing:

This was something that could work to their advantage.

One of them followed Arthur home.

The other man didn't have to. He already knew where Arthur Pinkney lived.

Inside the restaurant—which was called "The Europa House"—the maître d', Andrew, called one of the kitchen boys over. These boys cleaned tables, scrubbed floors, and generally ran errands. Andrew had a particular errand in mind.

He scribbled a note and handed it to the boy. He gave him an address and told him to take the note directly there, without stopping off for any reason.

"Give it to Orville Becker, George," he told the boy. "To no one but him. Understand?"

"Sure, I understand, Mr. Andrew."

George was a little simpleminded, but he tended to do exactly what he was told to do. That was why Andrew chose him for this task.

"Give it to Mr. Becker, George," Andrew said, "and I'm sure he'll have something for you."

And, Andrew thought, as George left the building, even more for me.

FIFTEEN

After dinner Clint asked Alison, "Where do you want to go now?"

She cocked her head to the side, thinking for a moment, and then said, "I don't know."

"It's your birthday," he said. "We'll do whatever you want."

She looked him in the eyes and said, "Anything?"

"Anything."

Suddenly there was a bit of commotion at the entrance. Clint looked over there and saw the maître d', Andrew, kowtowing to somebody. It was a tall, gray-haired man dressed impeccably in a gray suit. There was something familiar about the man.

"Alison?"

"Yes?"

"Does your father have gray hair?"

She turned in her seat, then turned back, her eyes downcast, and said, "Oh, damn."

"Just sit easy," Clint said. "There's no need to make a scene."

"You don't know my father," she said. "If he wants to make a scene, then that's all he'll do. It's when he's quiet, polite, and cold that you have to watch out for him—watch him closely."

As the man made his way across the floor Clint noticed that there were two men following him. They were both dressed in dark clothes, and their faces were expressionless.

"Who are the twins?" Clint asked.

She had time to say, "I don't know," and then her father was upon them.

"Alison," he said, smiling at her. Clint noticed that the smile did not extend beyond his mouth. His eyes were cold. He leaned over and kissed her. "Happy birthday."

"Thank you, Daddy."

Up close he could see why the man looked familiar. There was a strong family resemblance between father and daughter.

"Did you go to the theater?"

"Yes."

"Good."

Orville Becker looked at Clint Adams for the first time.

"Introduce me to your friend."

"Daddy, this is Clint Adams," she said. "Clint, my father, Orville Becker."

"It's a real pleasure, sir," Clint said, rising and extending his hand.

Becker hesitated, then took the hand, shook it, and said, "You think that now, but wait. Do you mind if I sit?"

"No, I don't mind," Clint said, reclaiming his hand and sitting back down. "Please, sit."

Becker sat down, made himself comfortable, then looked at Alison and said, "Darling, go and wait outside, in the carriage."

"Daddy—"

"Do as I say, Alison," Becker said.

She stared back at him for a few moments, but Clint could see she had no chance of defying the man—not in his presence, anyway.

"Good night, Clint," she said, dropping her cloth napkin on the table. "Thanks for going to the theater with me."

"I was happy to do it, Alison."

She stood up and left without looking at her father again. One of the two men went out with her. The other positioned himself just behind Becker's right shoulder. That put Becker between him and Clint.

"Alison is my only child, Mr. Adams."

"I didn't know that."

"If you try to see her again," the man said calmly, coldly, "I'll have you killed."

SIXTEEN

Becker started to rise, convinced that he'd had the last word.

"I think you'd find that harder than you think, Mr. Becker," Clint said.

The man stopped short and looked at Clint. He'd probably used that line many times before, and this was the first time it hadn't struck fear into the heart of the recipient. The man behind him moved, but Becker stayed him with an upraised hand.

"I beg your pardon?"

"Having me killed," Clint said. "It's been tried before, many times. Some men even came close, but as you can see, no one has yet done it."

"Young man," Becker said, even though Clint was probably only about ten years younger, if that, "do you know who I am?"

"Oh, yes, sir," Clint said, "I know who you are. You're a very important man."

"That's right."

"To most people," Clint said. "To me, at the

moment, you're just a foolish father."

Becker straightened and stared at Clint as if he were seeing some sort of strange creature for the very first time.

"All right," Clint said. "We've made tough noises at each other, Mr. Becker. I'm going to have another pot of coffee. You're free to join me if you like . . . or you can go."

Becker looked surprised. He had never been dismissed before. He sat back down.

The waiter came over and Clint said, "Another pot of coffee, and two cups."

"Yes, sir," the waiter said nervously.

Clint looked at the man behind Becker's left shoulder and said, "Why don't you send him away?"

Becker hesitated, then dismissed the man with a wave of his hand.

"Now," Clint said, "why don't we just talk like civilized men?"

"I'll have you checked out, you know," Becker said. He wasn't through flexing his muscles. "I'll find out who you are."

"You might find that you don't like what you find out," Clint said. "Why don't we just talk?"

The waiter came over with the coffee and the cups, left them, and hurried away. Clint did the honors and poured the two cups full.

"How did you know we were here?" he asked. "Was it Andrew, the maître d'?"

"That's right," Becker said. "He felt he was doing me a service."

"I see."

"Do you? Do you really, Mr. Adams? People *like* doing services for me."

"They're hoping for something in return, naturally," Clint said. "I mean, you're not foolish enough to think they do it because they like you, or respect you . . . are you? I wouldn't think so."

"I know why people want to do things for me, Mr. Adams," Becker said. "Tell me, what do *you* want?"

"I don't want anything, Mr. Becker," Clint said. "I simply went with Alison to the theater, and then took her to dinner. After that she would have dropped me at my hotel and gone home. In fact, she'd probably be home by now if you hadn't come in here."

"You know," Becker said, "you still have Arthur Pinkney to deal with."

Clint didn't respond.

"He's Gerald Pinkney's son."

"You've lost me," Clint said. "I don't have the slightest idea who Gerald Pinkney is. As for Arthur, I wasn't particularly impressed with him."

"You've met Arthur already?" Becker asked, looking surprised. He was obviously wondering what Clint was still doing in one piece.

"At the theater" Clint said. "He tried to get pushy, but Alison straightened him out."

"Alison can handle Arthur," Becker said, almost proudly. "I don't think you, on the other hand, would be able to handle him. He would break you in half with his bare hands."

"No he wouldn't."

Becker sat back and regarded Clint skeptically.

"Are you saying that you can defeat Arthur hand to hand?"

"No," Clint said, "I'm saying I'd shoot him in

the knee before I'd let him get near enough to grab me."

Becker looked surprised.

"That's barbaric," he said, "and cowardly."

"You call it cowardly," Clint said, "I call it smart. When you're faced with someone who is obviously stronger than you are, you don't let them get close enough to use that strength. I imagine you use the same principal in business, Mr. Becker."

Clint thought he saw something in Orville Becker's eyes then, something that told the older man that he might be facing a worthy opponent here.

"I think it's time for me to say good night, Mr. Adams," Becker said, standing.

Time to withdraw, Clint thought, and reconsider your enemy.

"It was . . . interesting meeting you, Mr. Becker," Clint said.

"Yes," Becker said, "yes, it *was* interesting, Mr. Adams. Good night."

Clint watched Becker make his way to the entrance, where he was met by Andrew. He said something to the maître d' that made the man stiffen and then nod. Becker patted the man on the arm and left.

Andrew, in turn, went and spoke to the waiter.

Clint called the waiter over and asked for the check.

"It's all been taken care of, sir," the waiter said.

"By who?"

"Mr. Becker."

"How nice of him."

The waiter withdrew.

Clint was glad Orville Becker had handled the check. He hadn't been sure whether he'd have to pay or not when Alison walked out.

He got up and walked to the front door. He stopped by Andrew, who looked at him and backed up a couple of steps.

"Thanks," Clint said.

"S-sir?"

"For a wonderful meal."

"Oh," Andrew said. "Yes, sir. Y-you're very welcome."

"I don't think I'll ever come back here, though," Clint said and left.

SEVENTEEN

Clint woke the next morning, went down to the lobby, ignored Harold behind the desk, and proceeded out of the hotel. During his walk the day before he had spotted a telegraph office, and that's where he was headed now. He needed to send a telegram to William Masters Cartwright, asking for information on Orville Becker. He doubted that Cartwright would want to send the reply over an open telegraph wire, but that was the Secret Service Director's problem. Somehow, he'd get an answer to Clint.

He found the office and sent a pretty clear message out. It said: REQUEST INFORMATION ORVILLE BECKER. Cartwright would know that the information was in reference to the assignment.

The clerk, having read the message back, looked up at Clint curiously.

"Send it," Clint said.

"Yes, sir."

Clint paid for the message, told the clerk what

hotel he was staying at, and gave the man some extra money to deliver a reply whenever it came in.

As he left he was reminded of what Becker had said the night before, that a lot of people "liked" doing things for him. Clint wondered if Becker would somehow find out about this telegram. Maybe it wouldn't hurt for the man to know that Clint had sent a telegram to Washington. The address, of course, said nothing about the Secret Service, but it *was* addressed to Cartwright. If Becker had Washington contacts, he could find out who Cartwright was.

Also, Becker would probably be spending a good part of this day running checks on Clint. He felt sure that when the man found out who he was—as Lieutenant Kelly had found out who he was—there would be another meeting between the two of them.

Returning to the hotel Clint saw a man coming toward him. It seemed he was going to become immediately reacquainted with one of the people he had met last night. The man coming toward him was Arthur Pinkney.

"Adams!" Pinkney bellowed.

"Arthur Pinkney," Clint called out, "of the Philadelphia Pinkneys, I presume. Did you follow me here from the hotel?"

"I didn't follow you," Pinkney said. "I was on my way someplace and I spotted you. But I'm not here to talk. I'm gonna break you in half."

Clint frowned. "Back off, Arthur," he said. "I'm not in the mood for this today."

"I'm gonna break you in half."

The man obviously had a one-track mind. Clint reached behind him and took the New Line from his belt. It was a small gun, but a bullet in the knee would still do some serious damage.

"Back off!" he said again. "Don't be stupid, or you'll walk with a limp for the rest of your life."

Pinkney took one step forward and then thought better of it. He stared at the gun, licking his lips.

"You're a coward," he said. "You won't fight me."

"You got that right," Clint said, "I *won't* fight you. We'd both end up busted up, and that wouldn't accomplish anything. At least this way, you're the only one who would end up hurt, and that suits me just fine."

Pinkney continued to look at the gun.

"It's your move, Arthur."

Pinkney pointed a thick finger at Clint and said, "All I want you to do is leave Alison alone. She's mine."

"She doesn't seem to feel that way," Clint said. "But I'll tell you what. You talk it over with her, and if Alison tells me that she's your girl, I won't go near her. Does that sound fair?"

Looking confused, Pinkney said, "Well, yeah . . . I guess so."

"Okay," Clint said. "Cross the street, Arthur, and keep walking. I hope we don't have occasion to meet again."

Pinkney stared at the gun for a few more seconds, then stepped into the street and crossed over. Clint watched him until he was twenty or thirty yards away, then heaved a sigh of relief and put the gun back in his belt.

He walked back to the hotel, checking behind him every so often to make sure that Arthur hadn't changed his mind.

When he reached the hotel he almost expected to find Officer Willis in the lobby, but the man wasn't there. In fact, nobody was there except for Harold, behind the desk, and Harold was making damned sure his eyes didn't meet Clint's.

Clint went up to his room and was fitting the key into the lock when he stopped short and took the gun out again. It wasn't anything he had heard, but rather something he felt, something it had taken years to develop, something that he always paid attention to.

Something that told him that someone was in his room. From past experience it was either someone who wanted to kill him, or it was a woman waiting in his bed. Both had happened to him many times before, and just to be on the safe side, he opened the door with his gun in his hand.

"Hello," Alison Becker said from his bed.

EIGHTEEN

He went into the room and closed the door behind him. He put the New Line down on the dresser with Alison watching him curiously.

"What was the gun for?"

"I had a visit this morning from your friend, Arthur," he said.

"Did he hurt you?"

"I didn't let him get that close."

She sat up, holding the sheet up to her neck. Clint wondered why women did that. First of all, they were naked in a man's bed. That was certainly no accident. Why, then, did they always hold the sheet up to their neck to hide the fact that they were naked? As many women as he had known, they still amazed him. Maybe that was what he loved about them.

"He didn't hurt me," Clint said, "and I didn't hurt him."

"What happened?"

"I convinced him to walk away," he said. "Alison, what are you doing here?"

"I wanted to find out what you and my father talked about last night."

"And for that you had to take off all your clothes and get into my bed?"

"I got tired," she said. "I wanted to take a nap, and I didn't want to wrinkle my clothes."

He looked around and saw her clothing lying in a wrinkled pile on the floor.

"I can see that."

"All right," she said, "I'll confess. This is where I wanted to be on my birthday night, right here in bed with you. My father ruined that."

"So you figured you'd kill two birds with one stone today, find out what your father and I talked about, and get into my bed."

"Right."

He walked to the bed and took the top of the sheet between his right index finger and thumb.

"Well, which one should we do first?" he asked.

She met his eyes boldly, then released her hold on the sheet so it was he who was holding it up in front of her. He opened his fingers and let the sheet drop down to her waist.

Her breasts were fuller than he thought they'd be. Dressed she looked slender, and she was, except that her breasts had some heft to them. They weren't large, but they were ripe. Her nipples were pink, and when he touched them they tightened immediately. She closed her eyes and took a deep breath.

He leaned over her so that she had to lie down on her back, and when he kissed her she came alive. Her tongue slinked into his mouth, and her arms went up around him. He slid one hand down over her smooth, flat belly until he had a finger buried in her, satisfying himself that she was not a virgin.

He left her then, long enough to get his own clothes off, and then joined her on the bed. Her hand immediately sought him out, finding his swollen manhood and closing around it. They kissed some more, their bodies rubbing. He put his hand between her legs again until she was wet, and then he slid one leg over her and entered her, slowly, cleanly. She was extremely hot and wet, and she lifted her knees and spread them. He slid his hands beneath her to cup her buttocks, and she gasped the first time he pulled her to him so that he pierced her deeply. After that she sighed each time he drove into her, and when her time was approaching she began to cry out, alternating between, "Oh yes!" and "Ooh, ooh!"

When he climaxed, she changed to, "Oh, God!" and said it over and over again until he stopped moving inside of her.

NINETEEN

"Mmm," she said, nestling up close to him later, "happy birthday to me! This would have made last night just perfect."

"And now?"

She kissed his chest and said, "It was perfect, anyway."

He slid his hand up and down the line of her bare back, enjoying the silky smooth feeling of her skin beneath his fingertips.

"Now the other part," she said.

"What other part?"

"What you and my father talked about last night."

"We flexed our muscles at each other."

"What does that mean?"

"It means he threatened me, and I threatened him. We did that until we decided it was a standoff."

She lifted her head and looked at him in disbelief.

"You threatened my father?"

"Well, I didn't exactly threaten him," he said, "but I refused to be cowed by his threats."

"What did he say?"

"He told me that if I ever saw you again, he'd have me killed."

Her eyes widened.

"I'm sure that's worked before," he said, "but I told him it wouldn't work this time."

"He must have gone crazy!"

"No," Clint said, "he got real quiet."

"I told you that's when he's dangerous."

"Well, I think he's going to check me out, get as much information about me as he can before he approaches me again."

"That sounds exactly like something my father would do," she said.

"Listen, Arthur's next move is probably going to be to talk to you."

"About what?"

"I told him that if you told me that he was your boyfriend, I'd leave you alone."

"Well, I'm not going to tell you that," she said. She slid her hand down over his stomach until she was holding his semierect manhood in her hand. "Not after this."

"Alison," he said carefully, "you do know that when I'm finished here in Philadelphia I'll be leaving, don't you?"

"Oh, of course I know that, Clint," she said. "I don't expect you to fall in love with me or anything. But you've shown me that I don't need Arthur. I'm attractive enough not to have to marry Arthur, aren't I?"

"Of course you are," he said. "What kind of question is that? Who ever told you that you weren't attractive?"

"My father," she said.

"What?"

She was silent for a moment, and then she spoke with her face pressed into his shoulder. She sounded like a very little girl.

"He was always telling me how I wasn't as beautiful as my mother," Alison said. When she closed her eyes, she could see her mother. "My mother was so beautiful when she was young," she said. She opened her eyes because she didn't want to see her mother anymore and continued. "She's dead now, but how could any woman hope to be as beautiful as she was?"

"You don't have to," he said, holding her tightly. "You only have to be as beautiful as you are. Believe me, that will be enough for any man."

TWENTY

Later, Alison got out of bed and started getting dressed.

"I have to go to work," she said.

"Your father doesn't know you work here?" Clint asked. He was propped up on one elbow, watching her get dressed. It never ceased to amaze him the pleasure watching a woman get dressed gave him.

"No."

"Where does he think you spend your days?"

She tightened her belt and looked at him.

"He doesn't care," she said. "I don't even think he thinks about it."

"Do you ever doubt that he loves you?"

She paused for a moment to think, staring up at the ceiling. When she had an answer ready she looked at him.

"I know he loves me," she said, "he just doesn't care about me, you know? He doesn't care what I do, or where I go."

"He cares if you see me," he said.

"That's because he wants me to marry money," she said.

"Like Arthur Pinkney?"

"Yes, like Arthur."

Clint started to shake his head, but he stopped when she leaned on the bed and kissed him.

"Mother cared about me," Alison said, "but she's dead. She died ten years ago, when I was fourteen. I think Daddy died a little then, too. I think that's what happened to him."

"I'm sorry."

"Don't be," she said, bouncing off the bed. "Not for me. I've turned over a new leaf. I'm taking control of my own life for the first time, and I like it just fine."

She went to the door, then turned and said, "Will I see you later?"

"Sure," he said. "I'll have dinner in the dining room. You can wait on me."

She made a face at him and said, "What about after that? Tonight?"

"I'll be here," he said.

She smiled at him, opened the door and left, closing it gently behind her.

Clint put his hands behind his head and stared at the ceiling. His next move had to be made for him. Either he'd be contacted by the informant, or he'd get a reply to his telegram that would give him some direction. Until then, he had nothing to do. He had time on his hands, and that was something he wasn't used to.

The watcher from across the street was back in his window, waiting and watching. He wasn't good at either, but he thought he was doing a good job at both. When he finally made his move, it would be a relief, but he didn't want to make it prematurely. That would be a disaster, and he definitely wanted to avert that.

The other pair of eyes, from inside the hotel, stared at a yellow slip of paper. It was a message, although not the one he'd been waiting for. Still, he had to act on it, and he hoped that his actions wouldn't put the entire assignment in jeopardy.

When Clint heard the knock on the door, he thought it might be Alison returning. That didn't mean he could get careless, however. He got up off the bed, pulled on his pants, took his gun from the holster on the bedpost, and went to answer the door.

The man in the hall was someone he didn't know, someone he had never seen before.

"Yeah?"

"Let me in."

"Why?"

"Because we can't talk out in the hall."

Clint stared at him. He was about thirty, clean-cut and well-built, casually dressed.

"Are you the man I'm waiting for?" he asked.

"I'm not the informant, if that's what you mean," the man said.

Clint frowned.

"Who are you then?"

"A friend," the man said. "I have the information on Orville Becker that you asked about."

"Jesus," Clint said, "Cartwright sent you?"

"That's right," the man said. "Now let me in before the informant sees us out here."

"What the hell?" Clint said, backing away to allow the man to enter. If Cartwright already had a man here, then what the hell was *he* doing here?

He closed the door, turned to the man, and said, "Start talking . . . and it better be good."

"Look," the man said, "I work out of Philadelphia. I mean, this is my regular assignment. When Cartwright realized that he'd be sending you here, he just told me to keep my eyes open and stay out of sight."

"He's taking a chance that the informant will see you hanging around," Clint said. "If that happens, my trip here is wasted, and so is my time. I won't like that."

"You haven't seen me up till now," the man said, "and neither has he. I'm good at my job, Mr. Adams."

"How good?"

"I saw you at the theater last night, and at The Europa. Today, you had another run-in with the big man from last night. You showed him your gun and convinced him to cross the street and keep going. Shall I continue?"

"Forget it," Clint said. "If you're so damned good at your job, why aren't you doing this one?"

"It's my understanding that the informant asked for you in particular."

"Yeah," Clint said, "that's my understanding, too—not that I understand it."

"Anyway," the man said, "I got the reply to your telegram."

"And?"

"And here it is," the man said. "You're to stay away from Orville Becker at all costs. Do not approach him again for any reason." The man wasn't reading; he was reciting. When he finished he looked at Clint, spread his arms, and said, "That's it."

Clint hesitated a moment, then said, "Shit."

TWENTY-ONE

The other man didn't quite know what that meant. He stared at Clint.

"That's shit," Clint said. "That's not the reply I wanted."

"Well," the man said, "that's the one you got."

"What's your name?" Clint asked, as it suddenly occurred to him that he didn't know.

The man was hesitant, but finally said, "Helm, Mike Helm."

"Look, Mike—can I call you Mike?"

The man made a gesture with his hands and shrugged.

"Mike, how much do you know about what I'm doing here?" Clint asked.

"You're waiting for some unknown informant to contact you and give you some information on . . . on a plot or something. That's what I know."

"Well, that's what I know, too," Clint said. "So now I happen to meet Orville Becker, a man who has contacts with the government. If you were in my shoes, what would you be thinking?"

Helm took a moment, then said, "I'd be wondering if he didn't have something to do with this informant. Either he's the informant," Helm said, warming to his subject, "or he's what the informant wants to talk about."

"Those are possibilities," Clint said. "It's also possible that he has nothing at all to do with the reason I'm—we're—here, but how are we to find out if I'm to stay away from him?"

Helm shrugged and said, "I don't know. How?"

"Well, luckily," Clint said, "I'm a volunteer here. I'm not subject to Cartwright's orders."

Now Helm's eyes got shifty.

"Hey, wait, but I am."

"So? He didn't tell you to stay away from Becker, did he?"

"No, but—"

"He told me."

"Yeah but—"

"And I'm going to ignore his . . . suggestion," Clint said.

"But—"

"But first I'm going to get the information I wanted myself, since Cartwright is obviously not going to send it to me."

"How are you going to do that?" Helm asked. "Where are you going to get it?"

"The morgue."

"The . . . morgue? What are you going to do, ask a dead body?"

"Not that kind of morgue," Clint said, grabbing his shirt and putting it on.

"What kind, then?"

"A newspaper morgue," Clint said. "What's the biggest paper in town?"

"The *Philadelphia Enquirer*, I guess."

"Then that's where I'll go," Clint said. "You can get a lot of information from old newspapers."

"I can't let you go near Becker, Mr. Adams," Mike Helm said.

"I'm not," Clint said, "not now, anyway. Besides, I never went near him; he came near me. Right now I'm just going to go and read some newspapers."

Clint started for the door, then stopped and said to Helm, "Your job is staying out of sight, right? You can't be seen with me or near me?"

"That's right."

"Then what are you going to do if I do decide to go near Mr. Becker?" Clint asked.

"I . . ." Helm said, and let it trail off.

"Think about that for a while," Clint said and left the room.

TWENTY-TWO

Finding the *Philadelphia Enquirer* building consisted of stopping a horse-drawn cab and telling the driver, "Take me to the *Philadelphia Enquirer*." Clint wished everything came that easily.

Inside the building he was allowed access to their morgue by their morgue attendant, who was only too happy to have someone to talk to.

"You know," the man said, "I know how they feel down at the hospitals, the ones who work with the dead bodies? Never anybody to talk to. I have the same problem here. All I have to keep me company is old news. How far back did you want to go, sir?"

"Years," Clint said.

"How many years?" the man asked. He was tall, with fair, thinning hair that made him look older than he probably was. While he could have passed for forty-five, Clint guessed that he was no more than thirty-five.

Something occurred to Clint then.

"Listen, do you maintain files on prominent citizens?" he asked.

"Oh, sure," the man said. "That's so our reporters don't have to go looking for old information when they're working on new stories. We got 'em on file right down here. What, uh, citizen were you interested in?"

"Becker, Orville Becker."

The man rubbed his angular jaw and said, "You wasn't kidding when you said prominent. Becker's as prominent as you get in this city. Some say he'll be running for mayor soon, and then even further than that."

"Governor?"

"President, even."

"That's interesting," Clint said, and it was. If Becker had political ambitions, it made it more likely that he'd be involved in some sort of political plot that was hatched in Philadelphia.

"Can you show me where that file is?" Clint asked.

"Sure thing," the man said. "Alls you got to do is keep it neat. There'll be other people using it, ya know?"

"I know," Clint said. "I'll keep it real neat—or as neat as I find it, anyway."

Which turned out to be not too neat.

When the man showed him the Becker file, it was already in a state of disarray.

"Look at this," the man said. "See what I mean? Now if the last person who used it had kept it neat, you wouldn't be stuck looking through this mess, would you?"

"That's okay," Clint said. "I'll try to straighten it

out while I look through it."

"Well, that's nice of ya," the man said. "That means I won't have to do it. You can use that table over there."

"Thanks," Clint said. "I'll probably be here a while, so don't pay me any mind, all right?"

"I won't," the man said. "I got plenty of old news to keep me busy."

Clint spent hours poring over the clippings in Orville Becker's file. It seemed Becker was a self-made man, having built his fortune all by himself from a very young age. There was no "old money" in Orville Becker's wallet.

There were also some photos of Jean Becker, Orville's wife and Alison's mother. Alison had been telling the truth when she said that her mother had been beautiful—and the photos probably didn't do her justice. Clint could see why losing a woman like that, at a fairly early age—she had been forty-one when she died—might drive a man deeper into his work. It was too bad losing his wife had driven a wedge between Becker and his daughter, though. Maybe there was still time for the two of them to fix that, but that would be up to them.

As Clint went through the files, he set them aside in neat piles. By the time he was done, he had several piles on the table. When the attendant saw it, he was very impressed.

"Hey," he said, "you wouldn't wanna come down here and be my assistant, would ya?"

"No thanks," Clint said. "I've got other career plans. Thanks for your help."

"Thank *you*," the man said as Clint left.

Clint decided he needed a beer. He went back to Dennis Collins's place and was greeted like an old friend.

"Glad to have you back," Collins said. "What'll it be this time?"

"Beer."

"Comin' up."

The little place was much busier tonight, although there were still some empty tables around. There were no girls working that Clint could see, and there was no gambling going on.

"If you're lookin' for girls and cards, forget it. This place is strictly for drinking."

"Looks like your policy doesn't keep any customers away," Clint said, accepting the beer.

"These are all regulars," Collins said. "I ain't gettin' rich or nothin', but I'm doin' all right. How you been doin'?"

"Not too bad."

"Seen the Liberty Bell yet?"

"No," Clint said, "I haven't had the time to see it yet."

"Better make time," Collins said. "You don't want to leave without seein' it. Oh, 'scuse me, I got other customers."

"Go ahead."

Clint leaned over his beer and thought about what he had learned about Orville Becker. He knew a lot about the man he hadn't known before—his educational background, some of his personal background, the huge government deal he'd made a few years back—but he hadn't learned anything that would really help him. Actually, the only interesting thing he'd discovered had come from the attendant, who

had indicated that Becker had political ambitions.
That had not appeared in the newspaper clippings.
Maybe Becker himself was keeping that stuff out of
the papers, and his plans were only getting around
through word of mouth.

"Another one?" Collins asked.

He startled Clint out of his reverie. He looked
down at the beer and was surprised to find that he
had finished it without realizing it.

"Why not?" he said. "That one sure went down
smooth enough."

"Good beer always does," Collins said. He drew
another and set it in front of Clint.

"You know, I'm a little surprised at the kind of
place you run," Clint said.

"Why's that?"

"Well," Clint said, being careful of how he put
it, "the last time I was here you indicated that you
could find me some action, if I was interested."

"And I can," Collins said, "just not here. I can set
you up with anything you want. What did you have
in mind, exactly?"

"Nothing really," Clint said.

"Women?"

"I can usually find my own women pretty well,"
Clint said. "I'm just going to finish this beer and get
back to my hotel."

"Back to your room, huh?"

"Well, I will be seeing someone after dinner."

"Ha," Collins said, slapping the bar, "a man who
gets his own action. You don't need my help, friend—
but if you decide you want it, I'm here."

Clint finished the beer and said, "Thanks, Dennis.
I appreciate it."

"You come back soon, okay?"

"I'll do that."

Clint left Collins's and started walking back to his hotel. He kept an eye on his back trail and was convinced that no one was following him.

TWENTY-THREE

Clint got back to the hotel just in time for dinner. He washed up in his room and changed his shirt. His hands and shirt had been covered with black ink and dust from the newspaper morgue. As he donned his last clean shirt, he reminded himself to have someone do his laundry. Maybe he'd talk to Harold about it.

He wondered idly if the police had questioned Harold again about his "black sheep" cousin's murder. He also wondered how they were doing on the case in general. He was almost curious enough to go and have a talk with Lieutenant Kelly about it, but he was concerned with how that would look. Kelly might wonder why he was so curious and become suspicious of him. He decided to just rely on the newspapers for his updates.

He went downstairs to have dinner, served to him by a multimillionaire's daughter.

● ● ●

It was time for Orville Becker to leave his office and go home. This was always the toughest part of the day for him. He was amazed that, even after ten years, he still dreaded going home to a house where there was no Jean. He knew that he should have been able to take some solace in the fact that he still had Alison, but the truth be told—and he would *never* tell her—he didn't like being around her because she reminded him so much of her mother. That was why when she left the house in the morning and returned in the evening, he never once asked her where she was going.

He was her father, though, and he still wanted the best things for her. He wanted her to marry money, and the Pinkney fortune seemed to be her best bet for that. It was too bad that, for all his size and ferocious appearance, Arthur Pinkney was such a . . . a *boy*! He had none of his father's acumen for business, and if and when the company fell into his hands, Becker felt sure that the boy would run it right into the ground.

Well, that was no business of his—unless, of course, Alison did marry Pinkney. If that came to pass, Becker would do his best to help the boy keep the business running. He didn't think it was likely, though. Alison was changing. The stunt she pulled with Clint Adams was proof enough of that.

Clint Adams! Becker still wasn't sure how he was going to deal with him. But one thing was for certain, he didn't want his daughter anywhere near the man known as the Gunsmith.

*   *   *

Clint entered the dining room and looked around for Alison Becker. He spotted her waiting on someone, and when she turned and saw him, she pointed to the table she wanted him to sit at. He walked across the room, seated himself, and prepared to wait patiently. At the moment Alison seemed to be the only waitress on duty, and there were several other tables taken.

As she walked past him she said, "I'll bring coffee right out."

"Slow down," he said.

"Can't," she said and kept going.

She brought him the coffee, and he drank it while watching her work. Knowing how much money was in her family, he was amazed at the amount of energy she put into her work. He was sure there were people with far less money than she had access to who didn't work a tenth as hard as she did. She was to be admired for what she was doing.

Still, he felt that if she stayed at home she might be able to bridge the rift between her father and herself. With him working at his job, and Alison working at hers, they'd never have a chance to mend their relationship. Untended, the rift would grow wider and wider, until they couldn't even see each other across it.

He knew she loved her father. He hoped that Orville Becker wasn't involved in whatever plot was supposed to be afoot.

At that moment a man walked into the dining room, and Clint recognized him. It was Mike Helm. As Alison showed him to a table, he never once looked Clint's way. For a moment Clint was thinking how foolish it was for the man to be there, but then he decided that Helm had a right to eat, too, and at the moment no one could make a connection between the two of them.

"What happened?" Clint asked as Alison came over to his table to finally take his order.

"There was supposed to be another girl working, but she never showed up," Alison said. She had a lock of hair hanging down over her forehead and looked frazzled and overworked, but at the same time she managed to look—well, happy!

"Just bring me a steak and some vegetables, Alison," he said.

"Okay, Clint," she said. She touched his arm and said, "I'm sorry I'm so rushed."

"That's all right," he said. "I have a lot of thinking to do anyway."

"Do some thinking about me, will you?"

"That's what I was going to do."

She smiled, said, "Liar," and rushed off to wait on another table.

Mike Helm was peripherally aware of Clint Adams in the dining room, but never once looked directly at him. It was probably foolish to come down here to eat, but he was hungry, and he hadn't known for sure that Adams would be here. Well, part of his job was to keep an eye on Adams, and he could certainly do that from here—without looking directly at him, of course.

Besides, the waitress was much more worth looking at than Clint Adams was.

TWENTY-FOUR

Clint was halfway through his steak when another man he knew walked in. It was Lieutenant Kelly. The man stopped at the entryway, looked around, saw Clint, and then started across the floor toward him. Clint saw the policeman give Mike Helm a cursory look, probably filing the man's face away for future reference. He did the same with all the tables he passed.

"Lieutenant," Clint said. "Nice to see you."

"Adams," Kelly said. "I'm sorry to interrupt your dinner."

"That's all right," Clint said. "Why don't you sit down and join me?"

"I'll sit," Kelly said, "but I had dinner already."

"Some coffee, then?"

"Sure."

Alison came over as if on cue, and Clint ordered more coffee and another cup for Kelly.

"Right away," she said. "Hello, Lieutenant."

Kelly hardly looked at her and nodded. Clint wondered where Alison knew the lieutenant from.

"What can I do for you, Lieutenant?"

"I'm stuck on this murder, Adams," Kelly said, "and I don't mind admitting it."

"How can I help you?"

"I don't know," Kelly said. "I'm just going over old ground."

"Do you want me to tell you again about my one contact with Les?"

"If you will," Kelly said. "I hate to make you go over it again, but I'm at a dead end."

Alison came over at that point with the coffee and poured the lieutenant a cup. He still didn't look at her, and she walked away.

Clint went over his contact with Les very quickly, since there wasn't much to it.

"Tell me again about the cousin, Harold."

"Nothing to tell," Clint said. "He warned me about his cousin."

"What kind of warning?"

"He said I should watch out for him, that he was the black sheep of the family."

Kelly tapped the fingers of his right hand on the table and said, "Well, that's it, then. I'm still at a dead end on this."

"I'm sorry I can't be more help," Clint said. "What about the people on the street who knew Les?"

"We've questioned everyone who knew him—that we're aware of, that is," Kelly said. "There's always a chance we missed somebody."

"Like the killer," Clint said.

"Yes," Kelly said, scowling, "him. You know what really bothers me?"

"What?"

"Motive."

"What about it?"

"There is none," Kelly said. "I mean, he wasn't robbed, he wasn't beaten, he was just shot in the heart at point-blank range. It seems—on the surface—a very cold act."

"Like something a professional would do?"

"Exactly," Kelly said. "And if Les was killed by a professional killer, we'll never catch him, because he was paid, did his job, and left the city."

"Leaving behind the man who hired him."

"Right," Kelly said, "except for one thing."

"What's that?

"Why would someone spend money to hire a professional to kill a nobody like Robert Lester?"

"Well," Clint said, "it seems to me that someone with a lot of money wouldn't see it as a hardship. I mean, the amount of money that was paid out would be nothing to someone like that."

"In other words," Kelly said, "I should be looking at Philadelphia's gentry."

"The high-society types," Clint said, "the wealthy businessmen."

Kelly's fingers were drumming on the table now.

"That gets touchy," Kelly said. "When I start questioning the wealthy people of Philadelphia, that's when the chief of police gets involved."

Clint shrugged and said, "It's your call, I guess. Maybe you just have to consider who the victim was, and if it's worth the effort to find out who killed him."

Kelly stiffened somewhat and said, "I don't look at who the victim was and then decide whether or not I should solve the murder, Adams. Someone was killed, and that's enough for me."

"Well," Clint said, "I didn't mean anything by it, Lieutenant. Like I said, it's your call."

Kelly looked down at the coffee that Alison had poured for him, then lifted it and drank it down. It had probably cooled off somewhat, but Clint still didn't see how anyone could drink hot coffee down that way.

"Well, thanks for your time, Adams," Kelly said, "and your input. Sorry if I overreacted a bit."

"That's all right," Clint said as the man stood up. "You take your job seriously. There's nothing wrong with that."

"I wish everyone felt that way," Kelly said, then added incongruously, "I'm married."

Clint nodded, as if he understood. Maybe the man was saying that his *wife* didn't understand his dedication.

"Sorry I interrupted your dinner," Kelly said. He turned abruptly and walked out of the dining room.

"What did he want?" Alison asked when she came over to the table.

Clint looked around. It seemed that most of the diners had been served and were eating, which was giving Alison something of a breather.

"He's having a problem solving a murder," Clint said.

"That man that was killed the other day?" she asked. "I read about it in the newspaper."

Clint looked up at her and asked, "How do you know who the lieutenant is?"

She looked chagrined and said, "I really shouldn't have said hello to him. Luckily, he didn't even remember me. I met him once with my father, at a reception of some kind. I'm glad he didn't notice me."

"Don't take it personally," Clint said. "He's got a lot on his mind."

"Well," she said, bumping into his shoulder with her hip, "as long as *you* notice me."

He looked at her again and said, "I'll notice you more later, when you're out of uniform."

"Ooh," she said, "I can't wait."

One of the other tables called for her then, and she hurried over, suddenly as engrossed in her work as the lieutenant was in his.

TWENTY-FIVE

Clint allowed Mike Helm to leave the dining room first, lingering over the last of the coffee until the other man had left.

When Alison came over to his table again, he asked her about Helm.

"Is that man a guest in the hotel?"

"The young man who was sitting over there? Yes, he's staying here."

"I haven't seen him down here before," he said.

"Come to think of it," she said, "I only saw him here once, before you arrived. Do you know him?"

"No," Clint said, "I was just curious."

"He's very good-looking, isn't he?" she said.

"Is he? I hadn't noticed."

"Aren't you jealous?"

"No," he said, "of course not."

"Why not?"

"Whose bed were you in earlier today?" he asked.

"Oh, you. . . ." she said. "I finish work at nine o'clock tonight. Where will you be?"

"I'm not sure," he said, "but let yourself into my room. I shouldn't be out much later than that."

"All right."

"By the way."

"Yes?"

"How *did* you get into my room this morning?"

She put her finger to her lips and said, "That's my secret," and hurried away.

Clint left the dining room and saw Harold behind the desk. The man avoided looking at him, so he walked right up to the desk and leaned on it. Harold had no choice at that point but to look at him.

"Can I help you, sir?"

"Harold," Clint said, "get someone to relieve you on the desk."

"Sir?"

"I want to talk to you."

"I, uh, can't leave the desk—"

"Get someone to relieve you for, oh, ten or fifteen minutes, then come out front and join me."

"I really can't—"

"When fifteen minutes are up," Clint said, "I'll come in and get you."

He went outside and sat down on one of the chairs to wait. At about the fourteen-minute mark, Harold came out the door, looking agitated. It was cool out, with a threat of rain in the air, and yet there was a thin film of perspiration on his forehead and his upper lip.

"I could get fired for leaving the desk," he said warily.

"You won't get fired," Clint assured him. "Sit down here."

"I'd rather stand," Harold said, "in case the hotel manager sees me."

"All right," Clint said, "stand. Tell me about your cousin Les."

"He's dead."

"I know he's dead," Clint said. "I'm the one you threw to the police, remember?"

"I didn't . . . d-didn't *throw* you to them," Harold said. "I was just answering their questions about who I saw him with last."

"While conveniently forgetting to tell them that you were his cousin."

"Well, I—"

"Look, Harold," Clint said, "if there's something you want to tell me in confidence, I won't tell the police it came from you."

"There's nothing—"

"The only reason you would have told the police about me was because *you* didn't want to talk to them," Clint said. "You figured they'd be too busy talking to me to bother you, right?"

Harold looked down at the toe of his right shoe.

"Harold?"

Harold looked at Clint and took a deep breath.

"Les said something to me the day before you got here," he finally said.

"What?"

"He said somebody was paying him a lot of money to pick a man up at the station."

Suddenly, Clint was very interested. If what Harold was saying was true, then somebody paid Les to pick him up at the station, and that meant they probably also paid him to bring him to this hotel.

"Are you thinking that whoever paid him killed him?" Clint asked.

"I'm not thinking anything," Harold said. "I just hope that whoever paid him—or killed him—doesn't find out that Les told me."

"Did he tell you who the guy was?"

"No."

"Or what he looked like?"

"No!" Harold said, growing agitated. "Look, he didn't tell me anything about the man, other than that he was going to pay him big."

"Well, he paid him big, all right," Clint said. "He killed him."

"And if he finds out I know anything, he'll kill me, too," Harold said. He was obviously a very frightened man. "Look, I have to go back to work."

"Go ahead, Harold."

Harold started away, then stopped and gave Clint a worried look.

"You're not going to tell the police I said anything, are you?"

"I won't mention you to a soul, Harold."

"Thanks, Mr. Adams."

"Thanks for telling me what you know, Harold," Clint said. "I appreciate it."

As Harold went inside, Clint sat back in his chair. If what Harold said was true—and he was inclined to believe the man, at this point—then Les's death was connected with his arrival here in Philadelphia, and probably with his assignment. The question now was, who promised to pay Les to bring Clint to this hotel and then killed him instead? Was it the informant, wanting to make sure that Clint got to the Holiday Hotel? Or was it someone else, maybe

with this assignment he was on—and consequently with a murder and a possible presidential plot.

She was kissing his chest, moving her mouth over him, down, down, until her tongue was wetting the swollen head of his cock. She moaned, opened her mouth, and lowered herself onto him. With one hand she held his testicles, and with the thumb and forefinger of the other around the base of his cock, she began to suck him.

He closed his eyes, giving himself up to the suction of her mouth, to the touch of her hands as she stroked his thighs and his buttocks and his testicles again, until he couldn't hold it any longer and exploded into her mouth.

Still later he held her while she slept, listening to her even breathing, wishing he had been able to find some way to tell her what he was going to do. That was impossible, however, because it would have meant telling her why he was here.

Resigned to whatever was going to happen, Clint turned his thoughts to Mike Helm. The man would surely be watching him tomorrow. What would Helm do after Clint left the hotel and he realized that Clint's destination was Orville Becker's office? Would Helm try to stop him, or simply report him to Cartwright? And what would happen then? Would Cartwright recall him? Hey, if that happened, he'd be only too glad to leave. He'd done his part for West, and for the government. He came to Philadelphia and put himself in danger. If they didn't like the way he was dealing with the situation, then they were certainly within their rights to recall him—and he'd be within his rights to leave . . . or stay anyway.

TWENTY-SEVEN

The next morning when they woke, they made love and then Alison left to go home. Her father would be at his office early, she said. She almost never ran into him in the morning, which suited her just fine. Clint wondered if she'd still feel that way if she knew that he would be going after her father in a couple of hours.

After she left, he stayed in bed about another half hour, then got up, dressed, and went down to breakfast in the dining room. One of the other waitresses served him, and he ate slowly, going over his plan. It wasn't much of a plan, admittedly. He'd get in to see Becker under false pretenses, supposedly to talk to him about his daughter. Becker would see him because by now he knew Clint's reputation and would be curious enough to see him. Once they were face-to-face, Clint would start his fishing expedition.

When he was finished eating, Clint noticed that Mike Helm hadn't appeared in the dining room. This was Helm's backyard, so Clint would have to count on the fact that he'd be followed to Becker's office. If Helm was as good at his job as he said he was, he should be able to follow Clint without being seen. What would be interesting was whether or not the man would try to stop him from contacting Becker.

Clint left the hotel. He had Becker's office address in his pocket. He'd gotten it from the most recent newspaper clipping he'd read about the man. In front of the hotel he waved at a passing horse-drawn cab, which stopped to pick him up. Once inside he gave the address to the driver, and then settled down to endure the ride. He was anxious to be face-to-face with the man. He forced himself not to look behind them to see if anyone was following.

When the cab pulled up in front of the address, he stepped down, paid the man, and then looked up at the building. It was a new, four-story brick structure, and he knew from his reading that Becker's company took up two floors—the top two floors. Becker also had an office on the waterfront, but he conducted most of his business here. Even Alison had told Clint that nine times out of ten her father could be found here.

There were two front doors, one which led to the main floor, and another which gave access to a stairway. Clint went in that door, still forcing himself not to look around for a tail. If Helm wasn't stopping him by now, that meant he wasn't going to.

He went up to the third floor, where he saw a door with the legend BECKER on it. That was all it said, as if anyone looking for Orville Becker *knew* what his business was. He knocked, tried the doorknob, and entered.

He found himself in a reception room. There was a woman seated at a desk which was situated directly in front of a large, plate glass window. She looked up as he entered. She was a handsome woman in her forties, wearing wire-framed glasses. She had auburn hair and lots of it, but at the moment it was all gathered up behind her head. She was wearing a suit and looked very businesslike.

"Can I help you?"

"Yes," he said, "would you tell Mr. Becker that Clint Adams is here?"

"Do you have an appointment?"

He smiled and said, "If you're his secretary, then you already know I don't have an appointment."

She held his eyes for a moment, and then a smile appeared, one that she had probably fought to keep hidden from him.

"Yes," she said, "you're correct about that. I am his secretary, and I do know that you have no appointment, Mr. Adams."

"And you've probably already heard my name, haven't you?" he asked.

She folded her arms on the desk top and said, "Yes, I have. In connection with Alison, I believe."

"That's right."

She appraised him critically, her head cocked slightly to one side, and said, "It strikes me that Alison might be a little . . . young for you—if I might be allowed to say."

"What's your name?"

"Brenda," she said, "Brenda Garr."

"Miss?"

She hesitated, then nodded her head and said, "Yes, miss."

"It strikes me, Miss Garr," Clint said, "that you're probably allowed to say anything you want."

"Ah, well . . . most of the time," she said, "but not always."

"Like when it comes to the boss's daughter?"

"Especially," she said, "when it comes to the boss's daughter."

"Well," he said, "why don't you tell the boss that I'm here to talk about his daughter?"

She stood up, hesitated a moment, and said, "Wait here, please."

"Where would I go?"

She started away from the desk, then gave him an amused grin and said, "You're not going to ask to marry her, are you?"

"Of all the things that I might be asking him, Miss Garr," Clint said, "that would be the last."

"Why? You don't like money?"

"I like money," he said, "it's marriage that scares the hell out of me."

She smiled openly now, obviously enjoying him, and then said, "I doubt that very much."

"It's true."

She studied him for a long moment and then said, "I'll be right back."

"I'll wait right here."

She was shaking her head as she went through a door which may or may not have led directly to Orville Becker's office. She returned in a matter of minutes and didn't speak until she had seated herself behind her desk.

"You can go in, Mr. Adams."

"Thank you, Miss Garr."

"A word of advice?" she said.

"Sure."

"Your sense of humor won't be as appreciated by Mr. Becker as it is by me."

"Really?" he said, heading for the door. "You appreciated my sense of humor?"

TWENTY-EIGHT

As Clint entered the office Orville Becker looked up from his desk. The walls were completely bare, no paintings, no tintypes or photos, nothing. The same went for the desk. It looked, for all intents and purposes, like an office where nobody worked, yet here was Orville Becker, millionaire shipbuilder.

"Please come in, Mr. Adams," Becker said. "Have a seat."

Clint came forward and sat opposite the older man.

"I must apologize for my behavior the other evening," Becker said. "I'm afraid I said some . . . some foolish things. I suppose I was trying to frighten you, but I can see now that you are not a man who becomes frightened easily."

"You checked me out," Clint said. It was a statement, not a question.

"Yes," Becker said, "thoroughly."

"Don't believe everything you hear."

Becker smiled and said, "I rarely do, sir, but if even

half of it—or a quarter—has any basis in fact, then you are a man to be reckoned with."

"I didn't come here," Clint said, "to be reckoned with."

"Here," Becker said, "meaning my office? Or to Philadelphia?"

"Take your pick."

"Why *are* you here, Mr. Adams?"

"Here in your office?" Clint asked. "Or in Philadelphia?"

Becker smiled grimly and said, "Let's start with my office."

"I wanted to talk to you about your daughter."

Becker frowned.

"What about her?"

"She loves you."

Becker folded his hands on the desk and said, "I don't need you to tell me that."

"You need somebody to tell you," Clint said.

"What is between my daughter and I is none of your concern, sir."

"Look," Clint said, "I'm not trying to . . . butt into your business, but I like Alison, and I don't like to see her upset."

"Why is she upset?"

"I don't think she even knows why, but I think it's because the two of you rarely see each other."

Becker fell silent for a moment, then said, "Well . . . I'm very busy—"

"You'll forgive me for saying so, Mr. Becker," Clint said, "but this doesn't look like the office of a very busy man."

"And what does it look like to you?"

"It looks like the office of a man whose business

by this time virtually runs itself," Clint said. "Do you really have to be here every day, Mr. Becker?"

"It is *my* business."

"Is there some reason you don't want to spend time with your daughter?"

The blood drained from Becker's face, and Clint felt that he'd struck a nerve with the question.

"N-no," Becker stammered. "Why would there be?"

"Tell me something, Mr. Becker," Clint said, leaning forward and watching the man closely, "I know that Alison doesn't look much like her mother . . . but does she *remind* you of your late wife, at all?"

Becker became very still, and Clint continued to watch him carefully.

"Of course she does," Becker finally said. "All the time. She moves like her mother did, she talks like her mother did . . . she has even developed a mind of her own, just like her mother did."

There was a long, awkward silence during which each man didn't quite know what to say.

"Maybe none of that is her fault, Mr. Becker," Clint finally said. "Maybe you should stop avoiding her like it *is* her fault."

Becker's face suffused with blood, and for a moment Clint thought he was going to lose his temper. He seemed to catch himself, though, and slowly the color of his face went back to normal.

"I don't think I want to discuss my personal life with you any longer, Mr. Adams."

"All right," Clint said, "let's discuss your professional life."

"I don't think—"

"Have you ever thought about entering politics?"

Becker stopped then and examined Clint through narrowed eyes.

"Why did you ask that?"

"I don't know," Clint said, "it seems only natural to me that a man such as yourself, who has accomplished everything there is to accomplish in his business, would look for other . . . arenas for his talent. Like politics, for instance. Tell me, Mr. Becker, what do you think of this country's leadership?"

Now Becker did become angry, as if of all the nerves Clint might have struck during their conversation, this was the most naked, the most raw.

Becker slapped his hand down on the top of his desk with a bang.

"That's enough," he said. "I won't have this discussion with you any longer."

Clint stood up and said, "My question about politics seems to have disturbed you more than any of my questions about your personal life, Mr. Becker. I wonder why that should be?"

"Get out, Adams!" Becker said. "Out, I say!"

The man started to look around, as if seeking something to throw, but the office was so empty there wasn't anything. Clint decided to leave before Becker decided on a nearby lamp. He'd got what he had come for, after all. Politics obviously was in Becker's future, or the question wouldn't have bothered him so much.

"I'm leaving, Mr. Becker," Clint said. "But I have the feeling you and I haven't seen the last of each other."

"Adams," Becker said evenly, "I have the feeling you are correct—and that if we do meet again, *one* of us is going to regret it."

Clint didn't have a line that would top that one, so he turned and left without saying anything further.

Outside Brenda Garr stared at him through wide eyes that were distorted just slightly by her eyeglasses.

"He's upset?"

Clint nodded and said, "He's upset." He shrugged and added, "It must have been my sense of humor."

She smiled sadly and said, "I told you so."

TWENTY-NINE

When Mike Helm saw Clint Adams enter Orville Becker's building he couldn't believe his eyes. He should have moved earlier to intercept Adams, but somehow he just didn't believe that the man would actually disregard what William Masters Cartwright had said and go and see Becker.

Once Clint Adams entered the building, Helm knew he was in trouble. He was going to have to explain to his superior how he had let Adams bother Becker.

Helm waited across the street from the building, and the longer Clint Adams stayed inside, the angrier he got at the man for putting him in this situation. He didn't understand why Cartwright couldn't have entrusted *him* with this assignment, even though the informant had requested the involvement of Clint Adams. Cartwright should have put his foot down. If the informant wanted to talk to someone, it *should* have been a regular member of the service, not some outsider.

If Cartwright had any nerve at all, that's what he would have done. This service would be run very differently once Michael Helm worked his way up to the directorship. The President could depend on that.

The man in the window across from the Holiday Hotel watched as the desk clerk, Harold, left work for the day. He knew which way Harold went when he walked home, so he took his time going down the stairs.

Thinking more about killing Harold, it suddenly made more sense to the man to go ahead and do it. It was likely the police would then think it was some *family* thing, something that someone had against the family of the two dead men. That would throw them off the track completely and leave the man free to do what he had to do.

When the man came out onto the street, Harold was already two blocks ahead of him, but that didn't worry the man. It didn't even worry him that Harold seemed to be walking a little faster today, as if he wanted to get home sooner than usual. The man simply started walking in the same direction. He already knew where he wanted to catch up to Harold, and what he was going to do when he did.

Harold didn't know it, but he was never going to get home that evening.

THIRTY

Clint had left Orville Becker's office and was standing out front when Brenda Garr came rushing out. When she saw him still standing there she stopped short and blushed, embarrassed to have been caught chasing after him.

"Hurrying somewhere, Miss Garr?" he asked.

"Actually—" she said, and then stopped short. He admired her for squaring her jaw and deciding not to lie. "Actually, I was trying to catch up to you."

"Why is that?"

"Well, Mr. Becker—when he's upset—isn't a lot of fun to be around. I thought perhaps we could . . . have a cup of coffee?"

"Sure, Miss Garr," Clint said, "but under one condition."

She frowned.

"What's that?"

"You have to call me Clint."

She visibly relaxed—he couldn't imagine what she

120

thought the condition was going to be—and smiled at him.

"All right, Clint, as long as you call me Brenda," she said.

"Do you know a nice place to have coffee around here, Brenda?"

"Actually, I do," she said. "I usually have lunch there."

"Lead the way, then."

Given enough time to think it over, he probably would have gone back inside himself and invited her for coffee or lunch. In business who knew more about the boss than his secretary?

She led him to a small café about three blocks away where they seemed to know her. The portly waitress, who had to be in her fifties, greeted Brenda warmly and told her to take her usual table.

"A little early for lunch, isn't it?"

"We'll just have coffee right now, Hilda," Brenda said.

"Sure," Hilda said, giving Brenda a wink that Clint was meant to see.

"She's a dear," Brenda said. "Next time I'm in here she'll want to know all about you."

"And what will you tell her?"

Brenda put her elbow on the table and her chin in her palm and said, "Whatever I learn today, I guess."

"Oh, that won't be much."

"It won't?"

"Uh-uh."

"Why not?"

"I don't like talking about myself."

"Why not?"

"I know everything I'll hear," he said. "I get bored. Besides, your boss knows all about me. That probably means that you do, too."

"He didn't show me the file."

"Oh, there's a file?"

She nodded.

"A thick one."

Hilda came then with a pot of coffee and two cups. She poured the two cups full and then withdrew, giving Brenda another look.

"And you didn't read it?"

"Well," she said, "I might have . . . glanced at it."

"Oh," he said, suddenly realizing why she wanted to have coffee with him. "You want to know if all the stories are true, huh?"

"No," she said, sitting back as if he'd pushed her, "no, no, that's not it at all. I, uh, oh . . . I don't know how to explain what I was thinking without totally embarrassing myself."

"Try."

She gave him a look and said, "You're not going to make this easy, are you?"

He sat back, folded his arms, and gave her an amused look.

"Well . . . I liked you . . . when you came in, I mean," she said haltingly, "and it occurred to me after you'd left that I might never see you again. Did you ever feel that way about someone? That if you let them walk away you'd never see them again, and then you'd . . . well, you'd just never know."

"Never know what?"

"Never know . . . you know."

He picked up his cup, sipped some coffee, set it down, and said, "This is good coffee."

"Ooh," she said and glared at him, but she could only hold the glare for a few moments before she dissolved into laughter. He soon joined her.

"All right," he said after they had stopped laughing, "I'll make it easier on you. Yes, I am attracted to you. I think you're extremely lovely."

"But . . . you're seeing Alison, right?"

"Alison is a nice girl," he said, "but I think she's got some problems with her father she should be straightening out."

"Oh, her father," Brenda said. "I could tell you stories, believe me."

"Really?" Clint said. He couldn't believe his luck and had to play this carefully. Putting on as innocent a look as he could, he asked, "Like what?"

THIRTY-ONE

When Clint Adams walked off with the woman Mike Helm recognized as Orville Becker's secretary, Helm couldn't believe it. How had Adams gotten her to agree to leave work and go off with him? If Adams was looking for some kind of dirt on Becker, who better to ask than the man's own secretary?

Helm had planned to approach Clint Adams when he came out, but now he decided to simply follow the two of them instead.

As it turned out, while she was a reasonably intelligent woman, Brenda Garr was also something of a gossip. She was only too happy to tell Clint stories about her boss, but to his disappointment, most of them had to do with the shipping business. True, Orville Becker had resorted to some underhanded and otherwise dubious tactics in some of his business dealings, but Brenda told him nothing that could connect the man to anything political.

So after they had gone through two pots of coffee and moved on to an early lunch, he asked, "What about politics?"

"What about it?" she asked.

"Well, don't men like Becker usually go into politics, sooner or later?"

"Well, there have been some men talking to Mr. Becker about that," she said.

Clint leaned forward.

"What men?"

"Oh, I don't know," she said. "Some group or faction . . . or are they a party? I don't know. All I know is they're trying to talk him into running for office."

"Are they being . . . fairly aggressive? I mean, does he need prodding?"

"I'm not sure," she said. "I've worked for him for five years, and I've certainly never heard him mention politics of his own accord. Not until these men came along."

"And you don't know who they are, huh?"

"Well, I remember one name," she said.

Clint tried to control his eagerness. What he did was not ask her the name. In that way, she was almost certain to come out with it.

"Angelo?" she said, prodding herself. "No, Angeles, that's it."

"Like Los Angeles?"

"Yes," she said. "His first name was . . . Henry. Henry Angeles. That's it." She looked at him then and asked, "Do you know him?"

"I'm not from around here, remember?" Clint asked. "How would I know him?"

"Oh, that's right," she said.

"Well," Clint said, "it's getting late. Won't he be looking for you?"

"Oh," she said, "it *is* getting late, isn't it? Well, let me write down my address for you." She did so and handed him the slip of paper. "Now that I've made a brazen hussy of myself, perhaps if you get the time you can . . . call on me. I mean, before you leave Philadelphia."

"Brenda," he said, putting her address in his pocket, "I'll sure try," and he meant it. He wouldn't have minded seeing Brenda Garr again—under the right circumstances.

Outside the café he told her that he would not walk her back, lest Becker see them together. If he had calmed down by now, they shouldn't risk getting him all upset again.

She agreed, said that she hoped he would call on her, and then walked away. He watched her as she walked up the street, until she turned the corner and disappeared.

"Jesus Christ," a voice said from behind him. "What the hell are you playing at?"

Clint turned and saw Mike Helm standing there, obviously agitated.

"Just the man I was looking for," he said. "Do you know somebody named Henry Angeles?"

THIRTY-TWO

They decided to get off the street before they were seen together, and ended up going back into the café Clint and Brenda had just come out of.

"Back so soon?" Hilda asked.

"Couldn't stay away from your coffee," Clint said.

"One or two?"

"One," Helm said.

"Two," Clint said.

"I'll bring two," Hilda said, leaving their table.

Helm asked, "Where did you hear that name?"

"Henry Angeles?"

"Shh," Helm said. "Not so loud."

Clint lowered his voice and asked, "Who *is* Henry Angeles?"

Helm leaned close and said, "The people in this city call him the President Maker."

"What?"

"They feel that he can *make* the next president of the United States," Helm said. "He's a powerful

127

man, wealthy and with a lot of influence. Where did you hear his name?"

"I heard it in connection with Orville Becker," Clint said.

"From his secretary?"

Clint nodded.

"Jesus," Helm said, "if *she's* seen them together, there must be something to the rumors."

"What rumors?"

"That Becker will be running for president."

"President?" Clint asked. "Shouldn't he start small? Like mayor? Or governor?"

Helm shook his head.

"Orville Becker has never done anything small," Helm said. "He'll try to go straight to the top."

"Then I don't understand Cartwright wanting me to stay away from him," Clint said. "If he's going to try for the presidency, doesn't that make it likely that he's behind this . . . plot, or whatever it is we're talking about? Why keep me away?"

Helm looked at Clint as one would look at a child who asked, "What is black?"

"It's *because* he is wealthy and powerful and possibly politically motivated that Mr. Cartwright wanted you to stay away from him."

"That doesn't make sense."

"You're not equipped to deal with that kind of a person," Helm said.

"And you are?"

"Truthfully? No," Helm said, "but at least I understand the need for someone who *is*."

"I think I understand," Clint said. "I'm too . . . aggressive. You need someone who will kowtow, bow and scrape, kiss their feet—"

Helm held up his hands and said, "I understand what you're saying, Adams, and to you it's probably true. You don't like politics, do you?"

"No, I don't," Clint said, "and I don't like politicians."

"Then there's no hope that you'd understand," Helm said, "but—if you were a member of the service—you'd have to obey."

"And since I'm not," Clint said, "I haven't obeyed."

"And you've put me in a bad position," Helm said. "I should report your actions to Cartwright— *Mr.* Cartwright."

"So go ahead."

"You don't care?"

"Not at all," Clint said. "Cartwright and I have had our run-ins before, and we'll have more. It doesn't bother me what he thinks of me."

"And what do you think of him?"

"To put it simply," Clint said, "I think the man is a waste of space."

Helm held his gaze for a moment, then sat back and looked relieved.

"I was wondering . . . if I was the only one who felt that way," he said. "I've met him once or twice, but I've been here most of the time I've been in the service. In fact, I'm not really a Secret Service agent— not the way someone like Jim West is."

"Then what are you?" Clint asked.

Helm smiled and said, "Well, to put it simply, I guess I'm a politician."

Clint stared across the table at the man for a few moments and then said, "You have my sympathy."

Helm took no offense.

"I know the way many people feel about politicians," he said, "but without them . . ." He let it trail off. Maybe he couldn't think of anything good to say about politicians any more than Clint could.

"Well . . ." Clint said, "what do we do now?"

Helm sat back in his chair and looked at Clint for a few moments before shaking his head.

"I may be crazy," he said, "but what the hell?"

"What does that mean?"

"I'm not going to tell Cartwright anything," Helm said. "You go ahead and do what you're going to do. I'll watch your back."

Now it was Clint's turn to study the younger man. Maybe Helm was realizing what a feather it would be in his cap if Clint did prove that Orville Becker was involved in a plot against the President. Cartwright would never give Clint credit for anything, but rather he would credit *his* man on the scene— Mike Helm. What men like Cartwright and Helm didn't understand was that Clint didn't want any credit. He just wanted to do what was right. If Becker was bad, he should never get into any high office. To Clint it was that simple. Here was someone Clint could keep from his goal if the man didn't deserve to achieve it.

"All right," Clint said. "I will."

THIRTY-THREE

When Clint got back to his hotel, Lieutenant Kelly was waiting impatiently in the lobby. Kelly was sitting on one of the sofas, his right foot crossed over his left leg, wagging nervously. When he saw Clint enter, he almost bounded to his feet.

"Lieutenant," Clint said. "Are you waiting for me?"

"We got another one," Kelly said.

Clint knew that "we" didn't include him.

"Another what?" he asked.

"Another body," Kelly said, "another killing."

"Who this time?" Clint asked.

"The other one."

"The other . . . what?" Clint asked, not understanding.

"The other cousin!" Kelly said impatiently.

"The other . . . you mean . . . Harold?"

"Yes," Kelly said. "Somebody killed Les's cousin Harold."

"But . . . why?" Clint asked.

"That's what I wanted to talk to you about," Kelly said.

For a moment Clint felt guilty. Had his conversation out front with Harold had anything to do with the man's death?

"Me? Why would I know anything?"

"You're staying here," Kelly said. "I thought you might have seen something, or maybe talked to the dead man."

Clint wondered if Kelly knew about their conversation—but no, how could he?

"Only to ask for messages, Lieutenant," Clint said. Kelly eyed Clint.

"Come on, Adams," he said. Suddenly the man wasn't as polite as he had been in the past. "After you found out that Harold gave us your name, you must have come back here and talked to him."

"Sure I did," Clint said. "I told him that I gave you *his* name. It was a childish thing to do, but I couldn't understand why he had given you mine. It didn't make any sense."

"Unless he was hiding something," Kelly said. "Unless he was trying to cast suspicion on you so we wouldn't look his way."

"Sure, if he was guilty of something, he'd be worried about that," Clint said, "but now he's dead. Did he kill his cousin and someone else kill him? Or was he killed by the same person who killed his cousin?"

Kelly rubbed his jaw.

"This is starting to look like a family thing," Kelly said. "I guess I'll have to talk to whatever family is left. Do you know—no, you wouldn't know."

"About their family? They're the only two I met. You better talk to the manager of the hotel. Maybe he can tell you about other family members."

Kelly scowled, as if annoyed that that particular course of action had to be suggested to him.

"I'll do that," he said.

"Lieutenant . . . I'm not under suspicion of anything, am I?"

"Only of being a stranger, Mr. Adams," Kelly said, "and I'm *always* suspicious of strangers. We'll talk again."

Clint watched as Kelly walked toward the desk, probably to ask for the hotel manager. He didn't wait to see what happened, but went directly up to his room.

Had someone been watching Harold and him on the porch? Was that why the man was killed, because someone thought he had told Clint something? And why wait until *after* Harold said something? Why not kill him before? Unless the killer didn't want to take the chance of committing two murders unless he had to.

And what about Kelly's theory? Sure, two cousins had been killed, but did that necessarily make the motive family related? Maybe that was what the killer *wanted* the police to think. Now the police would be pursuing that tack, and the killer would be free to . . . to do what?

Who was this killer, and did he have something to do with the informant? Was he waiting for the informer to contact Clint, so he could kill one or both of them? And if that was the case, why had he killed the two cousins?

There was a possible motive for killing Les. If the man had paid Les to pick up Clint and take him to the hotel, he would have killed him simply because Les knew him. That still didn't explain why he should kill Harold—unless it *was* to throw the police off the track.

Clint went to the window and looked out. There was no one standing on the street or in a doorway watching the hotel, but the killer wouldn't want to be that obvious, would he? Clint looked at the building across the street. It was three stories high, and he noticed for the first time that it was also a hotel. It was not as nice a hotel as the one he was in, but there were plenty of rooms with windows overlooking the street. It would be very easy for a man to take a room across the street and keep an eye on everything that went on—like a conversation on the porch.

Clint's eyes quickly moved from window to window. There were several windows where someone happened to be looking out at that moment, just as he was no doubt not the only person in this hotel looking out the window.

That had to be the answer. The killer had a room across the street, and he was waiting for the informer to make contact. Did that mean that when Clint left the hotel, the killer followed? Wasn't Helm watching his back? Wouldn't he have seen if someone was following?

Clint realized at that moment that he had taken Mike Helm's word for the fact that he worked for Cartwright. What if he didn't? What if Mike Helm was the killer? He could have followed Clint to the telegraph office and intercepted the reply, then invented a reply of his own. By convincing Clint that he worked for the Secret Service, he could openly follow him around and Clint would never suspect anything.

Clint had to find a way to get out of the hotel without Helm seeing him so he could send a telegraph message to Washington and check up on the man. For that he needed someone who knew the hotel, someone who worked there.

Alison.

Alison would be coming to his room later that night. He could find out from her about a back way out of the hotel, which he could use in the morning. He could leave that way, and then return, and Helm would never know. Or, if the killer wasn't Helm but was someone in a room across the street, that person wouldn't see him leaving either.

Clint recalled then why he hated doing these jobs—these "favors"—for the Secret Service. Things got so damned complicated.

THIRTY-FOUR

He did not approach Alison with the question immediately. They went to bed first and made love. He tried not to think about the fact that he was investigating her father while he was bedding her. He probably didn't succeed, though, because shortly after they had finished, she asked him about it.

"Is there something wrong?" she asked.

"Wrong? Why?"

"I don't know," she said, snuggling against him. He put his arm around her and drew her warmth close to him. "You seem . . . distant tonight. Are you getting tired of me? Did you want me not to come tonight?"

"No, of course not," he said.

"Well, good," she said, "because I'm not tired of you—not yet, anyway."

He pinched her, and she squealed.

"So what is it, then?" she asked.

"I do have . . . something on my mind."

"What is it?"

"Well . . . I think I'm being watched."

"Really?" she asked. "Watched? By whom?"

"I don't know."

"The police, do you think?" she asked. "I heard about poor Harold. Imagine that? Two cousins being killed just days apart. Did the police talk to you about it?"

"Yes, they did."

"What did you tell them?"

"I told them what I knew."

"Which was what?"

"Nothing." Clint told her.

"Did they believe you?"

"I don't know."

"So you think they're watching you?"

"Somebody's watching me," he said.

"What are you going to do about it?"

"Well . . . I need to get out of the hotel in the morning without being seen."

"That shouldn't be hard," she said. "There are plenty of other doors besides the front door."

"Could you show me one?" he asked.

"Of course," she said, raising her head. "Now?"

"No, not now," he said. "Are you working in the morning?"

"Yes," she said.

"I'll come down for breakfast," he said, "and then you can show me another way out. Maybe through the kitchen?"

"That'll be easy."

"Anyone watching from the lobby will just think I'm having breakfast."

"What if you're being watched by someone who's in the dining room with you?"

"They still won't know where I'm going," Clint said. "By the time they figure it out, I'll be gone. Then they'll just have to wait until I get back."

"Clint?"

"What?"

"Are you in . . . danger?"

He hesitated, then said, "I don't know."

"You're here on some kind of business, aren't you?" she asked.

"Some kind of business, yes," he said.

"Something you can't talk about?"

"That's right."

"Well," she said, putting her head back down on his chest, "I won't ask you about it. I don't care about it. As long as you don't get hurt. . . ."

"I'm going to do my best to see that doesn't happen," he said sincerely.

"Good," she said. "Let's go to sleep. I'll go down to work earlier in the morning so I can talk to the kitchen people. We don't want them raising a ruckus when I take you into the kitchen, do we?"

"No," Clint said, "we don't."

"Okay," she said sleepily, "okay . . ."

In moments, she was asleep.

Clint doubted that she had gone home from the hotel and then come back to be with him. That meant that she had not yet seen her father since Clint had spoken to him that afternoon. He wondered, when she did see him, if her father would mention anything to her about Clint's visit. He wondered if the man had taken anything he had said to heart. He hoped so. He also hoped, for her sake, that he was wrong about Orville Becker. He hoped that Becker was just a wealthy, bored man who was being pushed into politics by a would-be Kingmaker.

Across the street the killer watched as the light went out in Clint Adams's room. He was becoming impatient. Impatient with sitting in a dark room at night, impatient with watching and waiting. He'd killed two people, but even that couldn't keep him from being impatient. He still had not seen the target he was being paid to kill, and as much as he was being paid to wait and watch, it was becoming increasingly difficult. Hopefully, by killing the desk clerk, he had managed to occupy the time of the police and they wouldn't be around the hotel so much. They'd be concerned with the family of the two dead men.

There was no time limit on this job, and he swore that this was the last time he would take a job like this. In the future, when he took a job to kill someone, he would make sure that there was no waiting involved.

Waiting was a pain.

THIRTY-FIVE

In the morning, as planned, Alison went down first, going to work even earlier than she would normally. Clint remained in bed, formulating in his mind the message he would send to Cartwright. He would have to insist on an immediate reply, and he'd have to wait right there at the office for it. Hopefully, Cartwright would adhere to his request, and Clint would at least have the answer to *one* question—was Mike Helm for real?

Having given Alison an hour head start he rose, washed, dressed, and went down for breakfast.

In the lobby he looked around. It was early, and the lobby was empty. Behind the desk was a man he had not seen before. For a moment he wondered if the man was a policeman. Would Kelly be that smart? To plant his own man behind the desk? Clint wasn't sure about the lieutenant.

He entered the dining room and saw that only one other table was taken, by a middle-aged couple who did not look up as he entered. Alison saw him and nodded. He decided not to even bother with the pretense of sitting down to order. He walked right up to her.

"Do you want to sit down?" she asked.

"No," he said, "let's get it over with."

"Follow me."

She took him into the kitchen, where he drew curious looks, but no one said anything. She led him to a back door and stopped.

"This lets out into an alley behind the hotel," she said. "There's a lot of garbage, but not much else."

"Alison, thanks for your help," he said, kissing her cheek. He opened the door and started out, then stopped and turned. "How do I get back in?"

"I'll leave it propped ajar," she promised.

"Good enough," he said. "Thanks."

She blew him a kiss as he went out the door.

The alley extended both ways to side streets. He went right, because that was the direction of the telegraph office. When he hit the side street, instead of turning right to Arch Street he went left, then made a right. He walked two blocks, then made another right and this time went to Arch Street. He turned left and walked to the telegraph office, past Denny's Saloon, Dennis Collins's bar, which was, of course, closed that early.

When he reached the telegraph office he entered and found the same clerk behind the desk.

"Back again?" the man asked. "Did you get that reply from the last one?"

Clint had intended to ask the man about that and was glad that the clerk had brought it up himself.

"It was picked up for me, wasn't it?"

"That's right," the clerk said. "Fella said he was a friend of yours. Did he give it to you?"

"He did," Clint said, "but this one I'm going to wait for."

"I hope it was all right to give it to him," the clerk said.

"He probably paid you, right?"

"Well . . ." the man said, lowering his eyes, "I could get fired if I said yes."

"That's good enough," Clint said. "Send this . . ."

He recited his message, which the clerk wrote down and then sent.

"You're gonna wait here for the answer?" the man asked.

"I'm going to wait right here," Clint said.

The man shrugged, sat at the key, and sent the message.

"It may take a while," he said after he had sent it.

"I'll wait," Clint said.

There was a wooden bench against the wall, and Clint walked over and sat.

He didn't have long to wait. The telegraph key chattered a couple of times without a reply, but finally the clerk leaned on the counter and said to him, "Your answer's comin' in."

Clint got up and walked over to the counter to wait. The man wrote for a very short time, then handed the reply to Clint, who read it. It said: HELM IS REAL.

"Thanks," Clint said, and walked outside.

Clint started back to the hotel, then decided to stop in at Denny's Saloon along the way.

"Hey," Dennis said, "my best new customer. Beer?"

"Yeah."

Dennis set the beer down in front of him and said, "You don't look talkative today."

"To tell you the truth, I'm not."

"Fair enough. Just answer me one question."

"What?"

"Have you seen the Liberty Bell yet?"

"No," Clint admitted.

Dennis shook his head and said, "You're a hopeless case. Holler if you need another."

Dennis left him alone and walked to the end of the bar.

The telegram should have put his mind to rest about Helm being genuine. He certainly didn't need that extra worry to occupy his time. Still, even though there *was* an agent named Mike Helm, he still didn't know what the man was supposed to look like. Maybe he should have asked for a description of the man.

Clint shook his head. He was adding to his problem by suspecting Helm, who had done nothing to make himself suspect. He finished his beer, waved to Dennis, and left.

He took the same circuitous route to the hotel and found the back door ajar, as promised. He entered and walked through the kitchen, once again attracting curious stares.

When he stepped out of the kitchen into the dining room, Alison noticed him right away and came over to him.

"Your breakfast will be out in five minutes," she told him.

He'd totally forgotten about breakfast. Now that she mentioned it, he *was* hungry. He decided that he had nothing better to do.

"Thanks, Alison," he said.

"Sit anywhere," she said. "I'll be right out."

He walked to an empty table and sat. A brief look around the room revealed no one he knew, and no one who looked suspicious. He decided to put his mind at rest for at least as long as it took him to eat his breakfast.

THIRTY-SIX

At the same time that Clint Adams was leaving his hotel by a back door, Orville Becker was nervously waiting for Henry Angeles to arrive at his office. He stared out his window, barely seeing the street below, which at this early hour was almost empty.

It was amazing to him. He was much wealthier than Henry Angeles could ever hope to be, and yet he gave lie to the myth that money meant power. He admitted—to himself, at least—that in the political arena, Angeles was much more powerful than he himself would ever be—even if he did manage to become president.

Angeles had sources of power known only to him that supported his manipulation of men—chosen by him—into political offices. This, he claimed, would be his first foray into the presidential arena, and he had chosen Orville Becker to be *his* president.

In the beginning Becker had been enormously taken with Angeles and flattered to have been chosen, but as time went on and he *listened* to Angeles, he began to worry that he had allied himself with a madman. If Angeles talked of possible *illegal* tactics, he would do so only when the two of them were alone together. If Becker ever entertained the thought of turning the man in to the law—local or federal— there would be only his own word to substantiate his story.

But when Angeles starting talking about *assassination* as a weapon, Becker began to despair. Angeles had never actually used the word. He talked around it, like someone dancing around a hat, but that's what he meant, all right, there could be no doubt of that. When that happened Becker started talking about the possibility of not running. But Angeles had laughed. If Becker decided to go against him and not run, Angeles made it clear—and again without actually saying the words—that he could ruin Becker's business, make his shipping empire crumble, with just a few choice words in the right places.

So Becker was left with a dilemma, one he was even now struggling with.

He turned as he heard his door open. As usual, Henry Angeles entered unannounced.

"Good morning, Orville."

"Henry."

Angeles was a small, almost dainty man. His size belied the power that he held in his small hands. As if to further point out his own lack of size, he always carried a cigar in his hand—possibly the largest cigar he could find—and he never lit it. He gestured with it, used it as a pointer, but never lit it.

He was a fastidiously groomed man, his hair always combed straight back from his high forehead, exposing the pointed widow's peak. Becker suspected that the man had his eyebrows plucked. His scent filled the room, that peculiar scent that was only his. It was something he wore, some concoction that he no doubt had mixed especially for him. Becker wondered for the hundredth time how he could ever have fallen under the man's spell—and yet he had, as had many, many others—but none for stakes as high as these.

"Sit down, Orville," Angeles said, taking his own advice and crossing his legs. He pointed the end of the cigar at Becker and said, "You look like a nervous man."

"I am, Henry," Becker said, seating himself.

"Tell Papa why."

Becker cringed. The man constantly referred to himself as "Papa," and to the men he had placed into power as his "children," even though most of them were older than his own forty some odd years. It was obscene that a man so young wielded such power.

"It's Clint Adams."

"The man you told me about," Angeles said. "This 'Gunsmith'?"

"Yes."

"Has he spoken to you again?"

"Yes."

"Is he pushing?"

"Oh yes. . . ."

Angeles twirled the cigar in his hands for a few moments, then nodded to himself as if he had just made a decision. He stared at the cigar, so that it appeared he was speaking to it.

"Don't worry about him anymore."

"Why?"

"I'll take care of him."

"But what will you—"

Now he pointed the cigar at Becker, who responded as if it were a gun. He fell silent and leaned back in his seat.

"Don't . . ." Angeles said pointedly, then lowered his voice and finished, "worry about it, Orville. I don't want you to be nervous. Just leave this matter to me. Is that all that's bothering you?"

"Well . . . there's Alison."

Angeles waved him off and said, "Your daughter is not my concern—unless she's a danger to the campaign?"

Orville Becker's blood froze. What would Angeles do if he did think that Alison was a danger to the campaign?

"No," he said, too loudly, "no, not at all."

"Then that's between you and her," Angeles said. "Anything else?"

"No," Becker said meekly, "nothing else, Henry."

"Good," Angeles said with satisfaction. "Then let's talk campaign . . ."

As the man started to talk, Orville Becker made up his mind. He decided that he would go through with his plan, no matter what the consequences were. He had waited long enough. As soon as Angeles left his office, he would act—finally.

At the same time that Clint Adams was entering the Holiday Hotel through the back door, Orville Becker was sending a messenger to the hotel, hoping that he was doing the right thing.

Clint finished his breakfast off with a final cup of coffee. He had taken his time eating, paying attention to his food instead of the turmoil that was going on in his head. Maybe by ignoring the jumble of facts, suspicions, and suppositions that were going on in there they would somehow work themselves out. But with the last sip of coffee, everything was still as confused as it had been before. Oh well, that would have been too much to hope for anyway.

"What will you do now?" Alison asked.

"Oh, I don't know," he said. "Maybe I'll finally go and take a look at the Liberty Bell."

She pouted.

"You said you would wait for me."

"What should I go and see, then?"

She thought a moment, then brightened and said, "Valley Forge?"

"Really?" he said. "Is there anything to see?"

"History, Clint," she said, "history. But you *will* have to use your imagination."

"All right, then," he said, "Valley Forge it is."

She smiled and said "I'll see you later."

He got up and left the dining room. Before going back to his room, he stopped at the desk to ask the new desk clerk about messages.

"Yes, sir," the man said, "I believe you have one."

While the man retrieved it, Clint looked around the lobby. There were a few people present, but none who looked like policemen. Of course, by this time Lieutenant Kelly might have decided to have someone watching him who *didn't* look like a policeman.

"Here you are, sir," the clerk said, handing Clint a sealed envelope.

Clint took it, frowning.

"Do you know when this arrived?" he asked.

"I believe it was while you were having breakfast, sir."

"All right, thank you."

His initial intention was to take it to his room to read it, but instead he walked to a nearby chair, sat down, and opened the envelope.

It was a printed note, written in a tight, clearly legible hand. It said: *Your wait is over. Meet me at Valley Forge at midnight. Washington's house.*

He refolded the note, put it back in the envelope, folded the whole thing, and tucked it into his shirt pocket.

Why couldn't the informant have chosen someplace closer . . . like the Liberty Bell?

THIRTY-SEVEN

The meeting place for Henry Angeles and his hired killer was an abandoned warehouse on the water-front. He arrived well ahead of his man, for whom he had sent a messenger. After all, he was the only one who knew that the man had virtually taken up residence across the street from the Holiday Hotel.

It was Angeles's plan to have his man watch the man from Washington—who turned out to be Clint Adams—and wait for the informant to make his move. At that time, his man would kill them both. Now, however, with Adams turning out to be who he was, and starting to push—and with Orville Becker getting nervous—it was time to change the plan a bit.

He heard a sound and turned to see the killer walking toward him. The man's name was Wilcox, and Angeles had used him before.

"Mr. Angeles," Wilcox said. The man was always respectful. "I don't think I should have been called away from the hotel like this—"

"Plans have changed, Wilcox," Angeles said, cutting the man off.

"How so?" Wilcox asked.

"You've no doubt grown tired of waiting?"

Wilcox shrugged and said, "You know me, Mr. Angeles."

"Yes, I do know you, Wilcox," Angeles said. "That's why I know you've grown tired of waiting. Well, rejoice, my deadly friend. The waiting is over."

"You know who the informant is?"

"No," Angeles said, "but I've decided that—if he does in fact exist—I will not be putting so much importance on him."

"Then . . . what do you want me to do?"

"I want you to kill Clint Adams."

"The man at the hotel?"

"That's right."

"When?"

"Tonight," Angeles said. "After dark. Follow him wherever he goes and kill him."

"What about the informant?" Wilcox asked.

"Don't worry," Angeles said, "you'll be paid the same for killing one that you would have for killing two."

"That's not what I meant," Wilcox said. "If I kill Adams, Washington will just send someone else."

"Then you'll kill him, too."

"And what if the informant decides to go to Washington?"

Angeles shook his head and said, "You should leave the thinking to me, my friend. If the informant had the nerve to do that, he would have done it already. No, whoever this rumored informant is in my ranks, he won't leave Philadelphia to tell his tale. Trust me."

Wilcox hesitated a moment, then said, "All right, Mr. Angeles, you're the boss."

"Oh, you remember that, do you?"

"Well . . . sure I do. Why?"

"Those other two murders," Angeles said. "I didn't appreciate those, Wilcox. You will not be paid for those, you know."

"I know that, sir," Wilcox said. "They were just to insure that I got to the ones that *would* pay."

"All right then," Angeles said. "Carry on."

Wilcox nodded, then turned and disappeared into the darkness. Angeles would wait a significant length of time there in the dark for Wilcox to get very far away before he himself left.

For Wilcox the waiting was finally over. Tonight he would stalk Clint Adams for the very last time, and savor the moment when he finally killed him.

THIRTY-EIGHT

Clint could understand why the informant would want to meet at night. Darkness was often the best cover—but why midnight? And why Valley Forge? That seemed to fly in the face of wanting to meet after dark. Wouldn't it have made more sense to meet someplace where there were a lot of people?

Perhaps the informant feared being recognized. Was the informant's face that well-known? Was Valley Forge the only answer?

Of course Clint knew the history of Valley Forge, the famous winter camp of George Washington and his troops. He had never been there, but the note made it clear that there was a house there that had apparently been used by Washington as either a residence or a headquarters—or possibly both. What Clint needed was to go there while it was still light and have someone show him where that house was, so he'd be able to find it at midnight.

Clint went down to the dining room at about three o'clock, passing through the lobby. He spotted

Mike Helm sitting in a chair, apparently reading a newspaper.

In the dining room he caught Alison's attention, even though she was busy, and asked if she could leave work early.

"Why?" she asked.

"I want to go to Valley Forge," he said, "and I need a guide."

"We could go tomorrow, or the day after," she said. "I can get the whole day off."

"I want to go today, Alison," he said, "and while it's light out."

"Why not tomorrow?"

He just stared at her, and she understood.

"Oh, I see," she said, "there may not *be* a tomorrow. All right, let me just tell my boss, and I'll be right with you."

"You won't get in trouble?" he asked.

"Hey," she said, "what can he do, fire me? I'll meet you in the lobby."

Clint went out to the lobby and looked around while he waited. There were a lot more people there than had been there in the morning, but he still didn't see anyone who looked like a policeman— or a killer. Then again, who was to say what they'd look like, or that they wouldn't look the same?

Helm was still "reading" his newspaper.

Clint decided that when he left the hotel that night, he was going to have to do so the same way he had left it that morning, by a back door. He didn't want to take the chance that the informant might spot Helm and not make contact.

Alison came out of the dining room and walked right up to Clint.

"Okay," she said, "Valley Forge, here we come."

He made a point of not looking around right then, but he wished she hadn't said it quite so loud.

Mike Helm stared at his newspaper and wondered what the hell Clint Adams was doing going to Valley Forge with a woman. For a moment—just a moment—he looked at Clint over the top of his newspaper, and then when Clint and the woman went out the front door, he rose to follow them.

Wilcox had never even entered the Holiday Hotel before this day, but there he was, sitting in a chair in the lobby, as well-dressed as a businessman, apparently passing the day quietly. This was his first close look at Clint Adams, who was standing in the lobby, obviously waiting for someone.

There was another man in the lobby who interested Wilcox. This man was sitting virtually across from him, apparently engrossed in a newspaper. However, Wilcox had noticed, during the entire time that he had been sitting there, the man had never turned the page. That was precisely the reason Wilcox never used a newspaper as a disguise. It gave you away more often than it helped you.

The woman Clint Adams had obviously been waiting for came out and announced to the entire lobby where they were going. Wilcox, watching Clint Adams's face closely, saw the twitch of his facial muscles that betrayed his displeasure—however momentary—with the woman.

Adams was not going to Valley Forge to simply see the sights, of that Wilcox was sure.

The man with the newspaper watched as Clint Adams and the woman left the hotel, then quickly discarded his newspaper and followed.

Wilcox rose and followed him, knowing that he still had one preliminary matter to take care of—and he didn't mind that at all.

THIRTY-NINE

Alison had been right when she had said that Clint would have to use his imagination at Valley Forge. All there really was to see were some old cannons and some hastily built wooden huts which had offered some shelter from the cold winter winds, but little else. It must have been hellishly cold inside, he thought, hunching his shoulders and shivering at the thought.

"Cold?" Alison asked.

"Not as cold as those poor bastards must have felt," Clint said.

"The house is over here."

As they walked to it, he looked around. Flat ground for as far as he could see, very little cover. Not much chance of anyone sneaking up on them—unless it was dark, which it would be tonight. He couldn't quite remember what the moon had been like these past few nights.

The Washington house was a small, two-story structure which had served as both the general's headquarters and his residence. The rooms were small, but the house most certainly would have been much warmer than anything his men had. Understandable, however, to the military mind. The military kept their officers as warm and safe as possible, for it was the officers who directed the battles, the soldiers who fought them. If the high-ranking officers consistently went into battle with their men, or were subjected to the same living conditions, the army would have had to constantly replace them. Strategies would then change from commander to commander, with no consistency whatsoever. How long would the Revolutionary army have been able to last if that was the case—or the Union and Confederacy, for that matter? That was the same exact reason a man like William Masters Cartwright sat in his office and sent men out into the field. Jim West would have made a much better head of the Secret Service, in Clint's opinion, but West was too valuable in the field.

They walked around inside the house for a few moments, then stepped out a side door into a covered area.

"What do you think of it?" she asked.

He looked around critically. It would certainly depend on who got there first, the Informant, Clint, or the killer.

"Clint?"

"I've seen enough," he said.

"There's more to see," she told him.

"No," he said, "this is what I wanted to see. We can go back to Philadelphia."

"What's going on?" she asked, facing him. "Are you coming back here?"

He looked at her and said, "Time to go back to the hotel, Alison."

"Oh, all right," she said, exhibiting impatience with him for the first time.

Instead of going back through the house they walked around it and away from it. Nearby he could hear a stream, but he couldn't see it. He looked around, wondering what else was around— or who else—that he couldn't see.

From a safe distance Wilcox watched Clint Adams and the woman enter the house, and then come walking around it. He smiled to himself. It amused him to think that Henry Angeles had pulled the trigger just a little too soon. Wilcox was convinced that Clint Adams was going to meet the informant tonight, near or inside George Washington's house. He would have laughed aloud, but the sound might have carried, giving him away.

From where he was, he could hear a stream nearby, but he couldn't see it. He did not hurry to follow Adams and the girl. The man had obviously seen what he had come to see. He'd be back.

Wilcox looked down at his right hand. There was dried blood on it.

FORTY

Clint stared down at Alison while she was sleeping. The entire ride back from Valley Forge she had been stiff and unresponsive. He took her to an early dinner that night and talked to her about many things—but never once did they mention Valley Forge. As the evening wore on, she thawed out some and began to respond. When they finally got to his room, she came willingly into his arms, and they made love. He found her anxious, even desperate, as if she felt—or knew—that this would be their last time together.

For any number of reasons, it might well have been.

Orville Becker was extremely nervous. For one thing it was very rare that he went out alone late at night to go anywhere, let alone the deserted Valley Forge. He also wasn't sure whether or not Henry Angeles was having him watched. He didn't know whether Angeles considered him that much of a threat. Actually, while he knew Angeles considered him good political fodder, he doubted that the man had any respect for him, personally, beyond politics or business. He probably would never expect Becker to do what he was about to do—if he could keep his nerve up and see this thing through to the end.

In the final analysis, Orville Becker really didn't even want to be President of the United States. In fact, he didn't even want to be president of his own company anymore.

It was eight o'clock when the pounding sounded on Clint's door. He had been about to get out of bed and get dressed for his midnight meeting at George Washington's house.

"What is it?" Alison asked.

"I don't know," Clint said. He was on his feet, getting his pants on. That done he grabbed his gun from his holster and told her, "Stay there."

He went to the door, opened it, and found Lieutenant Kelly standing there.

"Lieutenant!"

"Get dressed, Adams," Kelly said.

"What's wrong?"

"I have another murder, that's what's wrong," Kelly said.

"Another one?"

"Three," Kelly said, showing Clint three fingers. "Three since you arrived in town. You and I have a lot to talk about."

"Who was killed this time?"

"You're gonna tell me that," Kelly said. "Get dressed. You're coming with me."

"All right," Clint said. "Give me a minute."

As Clint dressed, Alison sat up in bed and asked, "Who could have been killed now? And why is he bothering you with it?"

"Because I'm a stranger in town, and there have been three murders since I arrived."

"That doesn't mean you did it," she said. "Any of them."

"No," Clint said.

"But he thinks you know something about them?"

"Yes."

She stared at him while he finished dressing and then asked, "You do, don't you?"

He leaned over, kissed her shortly, and said, "Stay here. Wait for me."

"When will you be back?"

"I don't know."

"But . . . you *will* be back, won't you?"

"Yes," he said without hesitating, "I'll be back."

He had thought Kelly would be waiting for him downstairs. As it turned out, the man was waiting right outside the door.

"Can't you tell me anything—"

"Just that *this* one is not related to the other two," Kelly said. "He's not a brother, or a cousin, even distantly."

"How do you know?"

"Because the other two—Les and Harold—were the only two left in their family. Once they were gone, that was it."

"Nothing on the family angle, huh?"

"That was a wild-goose chase," Kelly said.

"How about—"

"Save it, okay?" Kelly said. "I don't even know why I'm talking to you at all, Adams. You know something about all of this. I can *feel* it. Be quiet a while and think about what you want to tell me."

Clint started to say something, then thought better of it. He *was* better off using the time to think.

Kelly took Clint to a waiting buggy, and they rode about a mile or so away from the hotel to a deserted street. There were no lamps nearby, and the moon was a sliver, casting almost no light at all. He knew that Valley Forge would be pitch-black at midnight.

The streets were wet. It had rained. Clint was amazed at how the rain had fallen since his arrival. It seemed to rain when he was inside, and not when he was outside. He hoped that would hold true tonight.

"Get out," Kelly said, even before the buggy stopped.

Clint got out, followed by the lieutenant. He saw a cluster of men standing nearby and frowned as he saw something on the ground at their feet.

"Go ahead," Kelly said.

Clint walked toward the men, who had been deep in conversation until Kelly and Clint approached. When they saw their superior officer they straightened, and one of them tossed a cigarette away. The ash flared and then died when it hit the wet ground.

"Nobody's touched it, Lieutenant," one man said. "Just like you said." Clint noticed that it was young Officer Willis.

"Uncover it," Kelly said. "I want Mr. Adams to take a look."

"Yessir," Willis said.

"Who's got a torch?" Kelly asked.

Another officer stepped forward, carrying one. It cast a yellow light over the proceedings.

Willis leaned down and removed the cloth that was covering the body, just enough so that Clint could see the man's face.

It was Mike Helm. His throat had been cut.

"Now don't lie to me, damn it," Kelly said. "You know this man, Adams, and you know what's been going on. I'm gonna throw your ass in jail *tonight* if you don't talk to me."

Clint's mind was racing. If he was in jail tonight and failed to meet the informant the man might never get up the nerve to set up another meeting. Yet, if he arrived at the meeting with the police, the same thing might happen.

Whether or not they would ever hear from the man depended on what he told Kelly now.

"All right, Lieutenant," he said softly, "let's talk. . . ."

FORTY-ONE

Clint Adams approached George Washington's house slowly, cautiously. The informant's message had not specified inside or outside the house, so first he was going to look outside. By now his eyes had adjusted to the darkness, and he could see fairly well. He had not brought any kind of torch or lamp with him for fear of frightening the informant off.

Clint had narrowly made Valley Forge by the midnight deadline, having spent the better part of two hours with Lieutenant Kelly. It was now almost ten minutes after midnight. He hoped the informant was not a stickler for punctuality.

He walked around the house until he came to the covered portion on the side. He didn't know if it was called a patio. Probably not, given the fact that it had been a military station a hundred years and change ago. He did not enter, but looked in from where he was.

"I'm here," a voice said.

He recognized it, and started with surprise.

"I didn't go inside," Orville Becker said. "I guess I don't feel . . . worthy."

"Mr. Becker?" Clint said.

Becker moved away from the side of the house and approached Clint, who was able to recognize him clearly then.

"Are you surprised?" Becker asked.

"Frankly, yes," Clint said.

"To be honest," Becker said, "I am, too. I did not think I would have the nerve to go through with it."

"You're the informant?" Clint asked.

Becker nodded.

"Why did you request me specifically? Until a few days ago, we'd never met."

"If I was going to talk, Mr. Adams, I wanted to remain anonymous. Not so much for my own safety, but for Alison's. I've met William Cartwright and Jim West at political dinners. I had to pick someone who wouldn't know me. The time I met West he spoke highly of his friend Clint Adams who had helped out the agency on several cases. I remembered the name."

"But the incident with Alison at the restaurant?"

"I had no idea the stranger with my daughter that night was Clint Adams when I was summoned by Andrew. It was only when I arrived and Alison introduced you. I had to threaten you to keep you from endangering my daughter. But after that night, you, too, knew who I was. That's why I wavered so long in deciding to contact you."

"I see," Clint said. "So there is a plot?"

"There's much to tell, Mr. Adams," Becker said. "I'm not sure where to start. Maybe it all started— my road to this spot, right here—with the death of my wife."

"Mr. Becker—"

"Just stand easy," a voice told both of them.

Becker looked at Clint, whose face betrayed nothing.

"What's happening?" Becker asked.

"Just do as he says, Mr. Becker," Clint said. "This man has already killed three other men."

"That's right," Wilcox said, "and all to get to this point, to get to kill the two of you."

"You didn't follow me," Clint said.

"Sure I did," Wilcox said, "but not tonight. I came this afternoon, much earlier. I've been waiting down by the stream. Have you seen the stream? It's real pretty."

"No," Clint said, "I haven't seen the stream—or the Liberty Bell, for that matter."

"You should have," Wilcox said, "while you had the chance. Now, I'm afraid, you will never see them."

"That remains to be seen," Clint said.

Wilcox laughed, a sound that came from deep in his throat, like a cackle.

"What's that mean?"

"It means I didn't come here alone," Clint said.

There was a pause, and then Wilcox said, "Sure you did."

"No, I didn't," Clint said. "After you killed Helm today, the police came and got me. There was only one way I could let them allow me to keep this meeting, and that was to tell them about it. Valley Forge is surrounded, my friend. You've got no way out."

Another pause.

"Sure I do," Wilcox said. "I got me a valuable man, here. I'll kill you now and take Becker with me. Once

I get away, I'll kill him, too."

"No," Clint said, "I can't let you do that."

"How are you gonna stop me?"

"I'm going to kill you."

"Big talk for a man with a gun in his back," Wilcox said.

"Oh, I didn't say that I expected to come out of this alive," Clint said. "You'll kill me, but I'll most certainly kill you, too. After that, Mr. Becker can leave or stay, whichever he chooses."

"Look, mister," Becker said, "you don't have to kill this man. I'm sure Angeles just wants me."

"Shut up!" Wilcox said.

"Get ready, friend," Clint said. "I'm going to move now."

"Hey!" Orville Becker shouted, and he moved before either Clint or Wilcox could.

Clint watched, shocked, as Becker charged the killer. The man's gun went off, and Clint heard the sound of a bullet smacking flesh.

He drew his gun and turned in one motion. The flash of the killer's gun had barely faded when Clint fired. Wilcox was turning back to Clint, but not nearly in time. Clint's bullet hit the man in the hip, turning him around completely. He staggered away a few feet, bent over, trying to stay on his feet.

From far away Clint heard men shouting and knew that Kelly and his men were closing in.

Wilcox might have been able to slip away to try and evade capture, but instead of trying he forced himself to turn and face Clint. He brought his gun up, and Clint fired again. This time his bullet froze Wilcox in his tracks for a moment, and then the man fell over onto his back. Clint checked him to make sure he was dead before he went to check on Orville Becker.

He was leaning over Becker when Kelly, Willis, and some others arrived.

"Jesus," Willis said, holding a torch up high, "that's Mr. Becker."

"Hold the torch closer," Clint said, trying to get a look at the wound, which was in the man's right side. A little lower and he would have been hit in the hip, as Wilcox was with Clint's first shot.

"How is he?" Kelly asked.

"I can't see well, but I don't think it's too bad," Clint said. "Just rest easy, Mr. Becker."

"It hurts like the devil," Becker said.

"Bullets will do that to you, sir," Clint said. "That was a brave thing you did."

"Really?" Becker said. "I'm not accustomed to doing brave things. I wasn't sure that I did it right."

"Well, sir," Clint said, "you might have avoided being shot, but other than that, it was almost perfect."

"This one's dead," someone else said.

"That's your killer, Lieutenant," Clint said.

"Get a litter," Kelly told one of his men. He turned to Clint then as the Gunsmith stood up and holstered his gun. "When do I hear what this was really about?"

"Lieutenant, I'm afraid that will have to come from someone else," Clint said. "You might want to listen to Mr. Becker for a while, though—that is, if he's still willing to say what he came here to say."

"Oh, yes," Becker said, from the ground. He was now being supported by Officer Willis. "After all of this, I'm certainly not going to change my mind."

FORTY-TWO

It was late the next day when Clint walked into Denny's Saloon again.

"Beer?" Dennis asked.

"Yep."

Clint wouldn't be seeing Alison later—and probably not again, since he was leaving Philadelphia in the morning. That was okay, though. Alison was at the hospital with her father, who had talked quite freely to Lieutenant Kelly about what had been going on, mentioning the name Henry Angeles more than once. Father and daughter seemed to be on the verge of a breakthrough of some kind, and Clint had left them to it.

Clint had sent a telegram to Cartwright, telling the head of the Secret Service that his informant was safe in the hands of the Philadelphia Police Department. He smiled as the telegraph clerk sent the message, because he knew Cartwright would hit the ceiling when he learned he was going to have to deal with the local police. Cartwright always liked to "supersede" the local authorities. That would have been difficult in this case. Kelly had not been willing to let Clint go the previous night until Clint told him something he felt he could believe. That meant that Clint had to tell the man something that was somehow related to the truth.

"Enjoyin' your visit?" Dennis asked.

"It's over," Clint said. "I'll be leavin' tomorrow morning."

"So soon, huh?" Dennis said. "Get done what you wanted to get done?"

"Oh yeah," Clint said, "that's all done."

"Good," Dennis said, "good. And what did you think of the Liberty Bell?"

"Oh . . . that," Clint said.

"You didn't see it?" Dennis asked, raising his eyebrows.

"Uh, no, I never got to see it," Clint said sheepishly. It didn't seem likely now that he'd be seeing it with Alison Becker.

"Jesus!" Dennis said.

Clint watched in surprise as the man took off his apron, came around the bar, and started shooing the other two or three patrons out of the place.

"What's going on?" Clint asked.

"I'm closin' up early," Dennis told him, "and you and me are going to see the goddamned Liberty Bell!"

Clint opened his mouth to protest, but then decided, why the hell not?

Watch for

NEVADA GUNS

137th novel in the exciting GUNSMITH series
from Jove

Coming in May!

SPECIAL PREVIEW

*If you like Westerns, here's a special look at
an exciting new series:*

On the razor's edge of the law,
one man walks alone . . .

DESPERADO

The making of an outlaw—the legend begins!

The following is an excerpt from this new,
action-packed western,
available now from Jove Books . . .

The wolf loped through the brush, moving soundlessly over the sandy soil. From time to time it stopped, testing the air, scanning its surroundings, listening. It was an old wolf, had grown old because of its caution, because of listening, watching, never showing itself. There once had been many wolves in the area, but most were gone now, most dead, killed by men with rifles, and traps, and poison. This particular wolf had long ago learned to avoid man, or anything that smelled of man. And it had survived.

It was late spring; the sagebrush still showed some green. The wolf had been eating well lately, many animals browsed on that green, and the wolf browsed on the animals, the smaller ones, the ones he could catch by himself. There were no longer any wolf packs to pull down bigger game: deer, antelope. Life was now a succession of small meals, barely mouthfuls.

The wolf was thirsty. A quarter of a mile ahead a patch of thicker green showed. A water hole. The wolf could smell the water. It increased its pace, loping along, bouncing on still-springy legs, tongue lolling from its mouth, yellow eyes alert.

A thicket of willows some fifteen feet high grew up on the far side of the water hole. The wolf gave them a cursory scan. It raised its nose, its main warning system, and could smell only water, willows, and mud.

It was late enough in the season for the water hole to have shrunk to a scummy puddle, no more than a foot deep and twenty feet across. In winter, when the rains came, the water formed a small lake. One more look around, then the wolf dropped its muzzle, pushed scum aside, and lapped slowly at the water. After half a minute the wolf raised its head again, turning it from side to side, nervous. The water had claimed its attention for a dangerously long time.

Suddenly, the wolf froze. Perhaps the horse had made a small movement. Horses do not like the company of wolves, yet this one had stood motionless while the wolf approached, held so by the man on its back. The wolf saw him then, the man, blending into the willow thicket, mounted, sitting perfectly motionless.

A moment's stab of fear, the wolf's muscles bunching, ready to propel him away. But the wolf did not run. Ears pricked high, it stood still, looking straight at the man, sensing that he meant him no harm. Sensing, in its wolf's brain, an affinity with this particular man.

Wolf and man continued to look at one another for perhaps a half a minute. Then the wolf, with great

dignity, turned, and loped away. Within seconds it
had vanished into the brush.

The man did not move until he could no longer
see the wolf. Then, with gentle pressure from his
knees, he urged the horse out of the willows, down
toward the water hole, let it drink again. The horse
had been drinking earlier, head down, legs splayed
out, when the man had first seen the wolf, or rather,
seen movement, about a quarter of a mile away,
a flicker of grey gliding through the chaparral. He
was not quite sure why he'd backed his horse into
the willows, why he'd quieted the animal down as
the wolf approached. Perhaps he wanted to see if it
could be done, if he could become invisible to the
wolf. Because if he could do that, he should be able
to become invisible to anything.

The wind had been from the wolf's direction. The
horse's hoofs had crushed some water plants at the
edge of the pool; they gave off a strong odor, masking
the man's scent, masking the horse's. A trick old
Jedadiah had shown him, all those years ago . . . let
nature herself conceal you.

He'd watched as the wolf approached the water
hole, made one last cursory check of its surroundings, then began to drink. A big, gaunt old fellow.
The man wondered how the hell it had survived.
Damned stockmen had done their best to extermi-
nate every wolf within five hundred miles. Extermi-
nate everything except their cows.

He was aware of the moment the wolf sensed his
presence, knew it would happen an instant before
it actually did. He watched the wolf's head rise, its
body tense. But he knew that it would not run. Or
rather, sensed it. No, more than that . . . it was as if

he and the wolf shared a single mind, were the same
species. Brothers. The man smiled. Why not? Both he
and the wolf shared a way of life . . . they were both
the hunter and the hunted.

The wolf was gone now, the moment over, and
the man, pulling his horse's head up from the water
before it drank too much, left the pool and rode
out into the brush. And as he rode, anyone able to
watch from some celestial vantage point would have
noticed that he travelled pretty much as the wolf had
travelled, almost invisible in the brush, just flickers
of movement as he guided his horse over a route that
would expose him least, avoiding high ground, never
riding close to clumps of brush that were too thick
to see into, places that might conceal other men.

He rode until about an hour before dark, then he
began to look for a place to make camp for the
night. He found it a quarter of an hour later, a small
depression surrounded by fairly thick chaparral, but
not so thick that he could not see out through it.

Dismounting, he quickly stripped the gear from
his horse, the bedroll and saddlebags coming off first,
laid neatly together near the place where he knew
he would build a small fire. He drew his two rifles,
the big Sharps and the lighter Winchester, from their
saddle scabbards, and propped them against a bush,
within easy reach. The saddle came off next; he
heard his horse sigh with relief when he loosened
the girth.

Reaching into his saddlebags, the man pulled out
a hackamore made of soft, braided leather. Working
with the ease that comes from doing the same thing
dozens of times, he slipped the bit and bridle off his
horse, and replaced it with the hackamore. Now,

the horse would be able to graze as it wished,
without a mouthful of iron bit in the way. More
importantly, if there was danger, if the man had to
leave immediately, he would have some kind of head
stall already on his horse. When trouble came, speed
was essential, thus the hackamore, and the style of
his saddle, a center-fire rig, less stable than a double
rig, but easy to throw on a horse when you were in
a hurry.

The man fastened a long lead rope to the hackamore, tied the free end to a stout bush, then left
his horse free to move where it wanted. He allowed
himself a minute to sink down onto the sandy
ground, studying the area around him, alert, but
also aware of the peacefulness of the place. There
was no sound at all except the soft movement of
the warm breeze through the bushes, and, a hundred
yards away, a single bird, singing its heart out.

In the midst of this quiet the man was aware of
the workings of his mind. He was comfortable with
his mind, liked to let it roam free, liked to watch
the way it worked. He had learned over the years
that most other men were uneasy with their minds,
tried to blot them out with liquor or religion.

His gaze wandered over to his horse. To the
hackamore. He remembered the original Spanish
word for halter . . . *Jaquima*, altered now by the
Anglo cowboy. Through his reading, and he read a
great deal, the man had discovered that many of the
words the Western horseman used were of Spanish
origin, usually changed almost beyond recognition.
When the first American cowboys came out West,
they learned their trade from the original Western
settlers, the Spanish *vaqueros*. Matchless horsemen,

those Spaniards, especially out in California. God they could ride!

When the Anglos moved into Texas, it was the local Mexicans who'd taught them how to handle cattle in those wide-open spaces. Yet, he knew that most cowboys were totally unaware of the roots of the words they used every day. Not this man. He liked to think about words, about meanings, mysteries. He had an unquenchable hunger to learn.

And at the moment, a more basic hunger. There was movement off to his left; a jackrabbit, one of God's stupider creatures, was hopping toward him. The rabbit stopped about ten yards away, then stood up on its hind legs so that it could more easily study this strange-smelling object. Rabbit and man were both immobile for several seconds, watching one another, then the man moved, one smooth motion, the pistol on his hip now in his hand, the hammer snicking back, the roar of a shot racketing around the little depression.

Peering through a big cloud of white gunsmoke, the man thought at first he had missed; he could not see the rabbit. But then he did see it, or what was left of it, lying next to a bush a yard from where it had been sitting when he'd fired. He got up, went over to the dead rabbit. The big .45 caliber bullet had not left much of the head or front quarters, but that didn't matter. The hind quarters were where the meat was.

It took him less than five minutes to skin and gut the rabbit. He methodically picked out the big parasitic worms that lived beneath the rabbit's scruffy hide, careful not to smash them, and ruin the meat. Ugly things. It took another fifteen minutes to get a fire going, and while the fire burned down to hot coals, the man whittled a spit out of a springy manzanilla branch, and ran it through the rabbit.

It was dark before the rabbit was cooked. After seeing those worms, the man wanted to make sure the meat was all the way through. He ate slowly, trying not to burn his fingers. For dessert he fished a small can of peaches out of his saddlebags. His only drink was warm, brackish water from his canteen. But he considered the meal a success, not so much because of the bill of fare, but because of the elegance of his surroundings: the pristine cleanness of the sandy ground on which he sat, the perfume of the chaparral, the broad band of the Milky Way arching overhead, undimmed.

Yeah, he thought, pretty damned beautiful. He scratched his chin through a week's unshaven bristle. And reflected that his life was damned lonely sometimes. Well, that was a choice he'd made, way back, and he was a man who stuck with his decisions.

Still, it could get damned lonely.

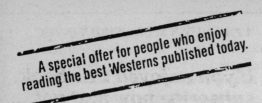